HARLEQUIN®

Temptation

EMILY McKAY

PERFECTLY SAUCY

"Sweet and sizzling..."
—*Romantic Times*

$4.50 U.S. $5.25 CAN.

HARLEQUIN®
Live the emotion™

www.eHarlequin.com

HARLEQUIN TEMPTATION®

AVAILABLE NOW:

#1009 BLIND DATE
Editor's Choice
Cheryl Anne Porter

#1010 HIGH STAKES
Tall, Dark & Restless, Bk. 2
Barbara Dunlop

#1011 PERFECTLY SAUCY
Emily McKay

#1012 REALLY HOT!
Getting Real
Jennifer LaBrecque

Jessica twirled a lock of hair around her finger. "Alex, honey, of course I want you—"

Alex inhaled sharply, his eyes darkening.

"To do the shot, I mean." Jessica grabbed a slice of lime from the bowl atop the bar and placed it on her collarbone. Unsure of what to do with the salt and shot glass, she held the shaker in one hand and the tequila in the other. Then she waited, squirming atop the wooden surface, trembling with a combination of anticipation and fear. She'd just manipulated Alex into doing a body shot off her in the middle of a crowded bar. If this didn't make her a wild, saucy woman, she didn't know *what* would.

Jessica almost felt proud of herself for making it this far, until Alex stepped closer and licked the side of her neck, his tongue—moist and hot—lingering lazily on her skin.

The room began to spin around her, and she shivered, arching toward him.

"You're sure this is what you want?" Alex's voice was low, rough, his breath hot.

Jessica swallowed hard, suddenly caught in a wave of panic. What was she doing? But then Alex's tongue pressed against her pulse point, and all reason and logic were swept away.

"Yes, Alex," Jessica said with a gasp. "I'm *definitely* sure."

Note from the editor...

An Evening To Remember... Those words evoke all kinds of emotions and memories. How do you plan a romantic evening with your guy that will help you get in touch with each other on every level?

Start with a great dinner that you cook together. Be sure to light several candles and put fresh flowers on the table. Enjoy a few glasses of wine and pick out your favorite music to set the mood. After dinner take the time to really talk to each other. Hold hands and snuggle on the sofa in front of the fireplace. And maybe take a few minutes to read aloud selected sexy scenes from your favorite Harlequin Temptation novel. After that, anything can happen....

That's just one way to have an evening to remember. There are so many more. Write and tell us how you keep the spark in your relationship. And don't forget to check out our Web site at www.eHarlequin.com.

Sincerely,

Birgit Davis-Todd
Executive Editor

EMILY McKAY

PERFECTLY SAUCY

HARLEQUIN®

TORONTO • NEW YORK • LONDON
AMSTERDAM • PARIS • SYDNEY • HAMBURG
STOCKHOLM • ATHENS • TOKYO • MILAN • MADRID
PRAGUE • WARSAW • BUDAPEST • AUCKLAND

ISBN 0-373-69211-0

PERFECTLY SAUCY

Dear Reader,

This is probably my last Dear Reader letter for Harlequin Temptation. I can't even begin to tell you what an honor it has been for me to write for this line or how sad I am for it to come to an end. Some of my all-time-favorite books are Harlequin Temptation novels. Books that are grown-up versions of my favorite fairy tales, like Janice Kaiser's beauty and the beast story, *Wilde at Heart* (#429), and Kate Hoffmann's ugly duckling story, *Love Potion #9* (#487). Books that made me laugh out loud, like Stephanie Bond's *About Last Night...* (#751). Books that I love because I felt a deep connection to the heroine, like Barbara Delinsky's *The Outsider* (#385) and Selina Sinclair's *A Diamond in the Rough* (#688). And finally, there are the books that I just plain love because they're so darn good, like Lyn Ellis's *Dear John...* (#488) and Donna Sterling's *His Double, Her Trouble* (#655).

These are the books that I've loved as a reader. For the writer in me, each of these books has raised the bar. Every time I sit down at the computer, this is what I aim for. I hope I reached it with *Perfectly Saucy*.

As always, I'd love to hear from you. You can e-mail me at Emily@EmilyMcKay.com or write to me at P.O. Box 163104, Austin, TX 78716-3104.

Enjoy,

Emily McKay

Books by Emily McKay

HARLEQUIN TEMPTATION
912—BABY, BE MINE
976—PERFECTLY SEXY

For my wonderful family. For my father, who taught me to do the right thing, my mother, who taught me how to have fun, and my sister, who is always there for me.

Prologue

10 THINGS EVERY WOMAN SHOULD DO
—Excerpted from *Saucy* magazine

1. Find Your Fling— After all, when was the last time you had an affair to remember?
2. Don't Be a Homebody— Fly away from your nest to live abroad.
3. Go Tribal— Get a tattoo or piercing to channel the wild thing inside.
4. Release Your Inner Dominatrix— Buy a leather skirt and wear it proudly. Whip, optional.
5. Be a Diva in Bed— Don't just ask for what you want, demand it.
6. Drop the Drawers— He'll go crazy when he finds out you're going commando.
7. Live in the Fast Lane— Relive the thrill of the forbidden by having sex in the back seat of the car.
8. Just Admit It— Own up to a big mistake. After all, confession is good for your soul and guilt is bad for your skin.
9. Shake Up Your Space— Because life should be shaken, not stirred.
10. Conquer It— Overcome your greatest fear and you'll know you can do anything.

1

ALEX MORENO was the first person Jessica Summers had ever heard say the F-word out loud. By the time she'd heard him say it in the eighth grade, she was fairly certain he'd already done…it several times.

Even at fourteen he'd had his pick of girls and the girls he'd picked were almost always older, more experienced and willing to do all the things Jessica only whispered about at sleep-overs. In high school he'd been the kind of boy girls fawned over, boys picked fights with and teachers disciplined just to prove they were in control.

Apparently things hadn't changed much. Two weeks ago Jessica had seen him for the first time in more than ten years. He'd been walking down the street with a kind of lazy confidence that declared he was back in Palo Verde to stay and there was nothing anyone could do about it, short of arresting him and physically hauling his ass out of town. Again.

Even after all this time, they were still polar opposites. He was the son of migrant farm workers. She was the daughter of the town's most prominent family. He was wild, reckless and brash. The ultimate bad boy.

She, on the other hand, seemed doomed to a tragically boring, spinsterlike existence. Unless she did something drastic.

Jessica glanced down at the delicate silver watch on her wrist. Four forty-five. Alex would be here soon and the next hour was going to go either very well or very badly.

Turning, she paced the length of her kitchen, the three-inch heels of her shoes *rat-tat*ing across the tile floor, echoing the pounding of her heart. She reached the arched doorway to her living room and kept going, the plush cream carpet muffling the clatter of her heels as she strode toward the sliding-glass door that looked out onto her back patio and pool. She stood for a moment, watching the surface of the water ripple in a breeze and wishing she wasn't perpetually early. Today, fifteen minutes seemed like an eternity.

Her telephone rang, its shrill clatter piercing the silence. She spun around, lunging for the cordless phone she kept on the coffee table, sure it was Alex calling to cancel their appointment.

Her heel caught on the carpet and she kicked off her shoes, nudging them under the table as she grabbed the handset. For a second she clutched the phone, exhaling sharply so she wouldn't sound like such a nervous wreck. Would she be disappointed or relieved if he couldn't make it?

Mustering her courage, she punched the talk button and tried to sound casual. "Hello? Sumners residence."

God, why did she always sound as though she was answering her parents' phone?

"What are you wearing?" demanded a feminine voice.

"Patricia?"

"No, it's your great-uncle Vernon. Of course it's Patricia." Her voice practically rang with exasperation. "He's going to be there soon, right?"

"Maybe ten, fifteen minutes."

"So don't waste my time with pleasantries. If you'd responded to my e-mails at work today, we wouldn't have to do this at the last minute. Now, what are you wearing?"

Jessica had made the mistake of telling Patricia over lunch about her plan to meet Alex this evening. The other woman had ignored work all afternoon, peppering Jessica with frantic e-mail questions. Most of which Jessica had ignored. "Why does it matter what I'm wearing?"

"You're going to see Alex for the first time in how many years?"

"Ten."

"And you don't think it matters what you're wearing?" She didn't give Jessica a chance to answer but plowed right ahead with the conversation. "Just tell me it's not one of your god-awful, prissy little sweater sets."

"No," she said through gritted teeth as she made her way to the entry hall. "It's not one of my practical and comfortable sweater sets. I'm wearing a simple black silk sheath dress."

"Is it tight?"

Jessica paused in front of the hall mirror just long enough to shoot herself a piercing look. "No."

"Is it low-cut?"

"No." She felt a sinking sensation deep in her belly. Had she worn the completely wrong thing?

"It's at least short?"

Jessica extended her leg to get a better look at the length. "Four, maybe five inches above the knee."

"Good. That's good. Your legs are your best feature."

Please, Dear God, let Alex be a leg man.

"Okay," Patricia barked, clearly moving beyond the clothing issue. "So what's your game plan?"

"Game plan?"

"What're you going to do? Just invite him in and proposition him?"

"No, of course not!" When she'd spoken to Alex on the phone earlier this afternoon she'd said something inane about wanting to hire his construction company to do work on her house. But she'd had no idea how she would segue from "Want to remodel my kitchen" to "Want to go out sometime?" Or, after a date or two, to transition to "Want to tear off each other's clothes and have mad, passionate sex? Often?"

To Patricia she said, "I just…"

"Just what?"

"I don't know." She spun on her heel and stomped back to the kitchen, suddenly irritated with herself. "I don't really have a plan."

"Exactly. *You* don't have a plan. That's what worries me. You *always* have a plan."

"That's not—"

"Did you or did you not just send everyone in our team a detailed plan of what to do in case of a tornado?"

"I'm the floor safety manager now. It's my job to—"

"We live in California. There are no tornadoes in California."

"But—"

"Ever."

She started to explain that she was just trying to do her job well. That she took her new responsibilities at work seriously. But wasn't that the problem? She always took everything so dang seriously.

Before she could put any of that into words, Patricia babbled on. "So, yes, it scares me that you have no plan. This is just so unlike you. Inviting Alex Moreno over so you can seduce him or whatever is just so…so…"

"Like something you would do?"

"Exactly. This is what concerns me. You are acting like me."

"Well, you can stop worrying. I'm not going to seduce or proposition him. I promise. I just want to see him again."

To see if any spark of attraction still lingered between them.

And if it did?

Well, she'd worry about that when the time came.

"See him *again?*" Patricia asked shrewdly. "There wasn't something going on between you two back in school, was there?"

"No," she said dismissively. And it wasn't entirely a lie.

"I didn't think so. I mean, I'd heard the rumors, but I never thought they were true."

"Rumors?" She'd certainly never heard any rumors connecting the two of them.

"That you were secretly in love. That you were going to run away together. I figured it was nonsense. I mean, you and Alex Moreno? It was more absurd than that rumor about the giant snake living in the second-floor bathroom."

"What's that supposed to mean?" she asked, more than a little offended about the snake comparison.

"Just that you weren't each other's type. You were such a Goody Two-shoes in high school. And he was always in and out of trouble. And on top of all that, your father was the judge. How ironic would that have been? The daughter of a judge dating a guy who'd been arrested at least a dozen times."

"Hmm. Very," Jessica said noncommittally. Of course, the real irony was that, although the rumors had been false, at the time, she would have given anything for them to be true.

"But I guess you must have had a crush on him then," Patricia continued blithely. "Or else you wouldn't be thinking of having your passionate fling with him now. Not that I blame you. He was scrumptious even at eighteen. And just so bad."

Patricia's inflection on the word "bad" made it clear she thought "bad" was a very good thing.

And Jessica supposed she knew what Patricia meant. Even a Goody Two-shoes like her could appreciate the thrilling appeal of being naughty. But that was never what had drawn her to Alex.

It wasn't his bad-boy charm, his many arrests or the titillation of shocking her parents and her peers. No, what appealed to her most about Alex Moreno—even now— was all the things about him no one else saw. His strength. His kindness. His integrity.

Well, all that and his sizzling raw sex appeal.

For now she needed to get Patricia off the phone before her friend's circuitous logic drove her absolutely batty.

But before she hung up, she couldn't help but ask, "What I don't get is this. If you're so worried about what I'm doing, why did you want to make sure my clothes met with your approval?"

"Well, sure, I'm worried. That's all the more reason for you to look drool-worthy. If you're going to make a fool out of yourself, I at least want you to look good while you do it."

Buoyed by Patricia's "encouragement," Jessica poured herself a splash of wine and gulped it down. "Thanks, that's very helpful."

"I'm sorry I'm not more optimistic." But Patricia didn't

sound the least bit contrite. "Look, I can understand you wanting to get some—I mean, lately you've been living like a nun—but, come on, Alex Moreno? Going from celibacy straight to him is like deciding you need to work out more often and starting by climbing Mount Everest."

"Pffft," Jessica muttered dismissively. But was Patricia right? Was Alex the Mount Everest of men? Was she insane for thinking he might be interested in her? Was she crazy for thinking he'd even remember her?

"Jess, you can 'pffft' all you want, but he's the baddest bad boy this town has ever known. You could get into serious trouble with a guy like him. And if you're doing this just because of that silly list…"

On her way back from a nine-week-long business trip to Sweden—a trip during which she'd worked her butt off and still hadn't gotten the promotion she'd been promised—she'd picked up a copy of *Saucy* magazine in Gatwick Airport. The cover article was "10 Things Every Woman Should Do." Have an Affair to Remember was at the top of that list. And Alex Moreno was at the top of her list of men she'd want to have a passionate affair with.

"Patricia, you only think The List is silly because you've done all of the things on The List."

"Well—" She chuckled, sounding just a tad smug. "I guess I have."

"Exactly," Jessica growled.

"Hey." Patricia sounded falsely cheerful. "It's not like you haven't done *any* of the things on the list."

"One. I've done one. Live Abroad. That's the one and only thing on The List that I've done. And that hardly counts since I did that for work."

"All I'm saying is," Patricia countered, "you want to do some of the things on The List? Fine. But start with something smaller. Something a little less traumatic. Less likely to come back and bite you on the ass. Why not buy a leather miniskirt? That was on the list, too, right? Or get a tattoo."

"Get a tattoo? You think permanently scarring my body would be less traumatic than sleeping with Alex?"

"Okay, traumatic maybe wasn't the best word. Drastic is more what I meant. I just don't think you need to do anything quite so drastic."

And that was exactly what Patricia—who'd done all the things on the list numerous times—didn't get. Drastic was just what Jessica needed.

"I've worked for Handheld Technologies for six years now," she pointed out. "For the past two years, I've been working my butt off for a promotion to team leader. Instead of promoting me, they made me floor safety manager—the schmuck in charge of keeping the first-aid kit stocked and evacuating the floor in case of a natural disaster."

"It's almost like a promotion," Patricia murmured in placating tones. "It's a sign they trust you."

"No, it's a sign they think I'll look okay in a bright orange vest. I'm tired of settling for floor safety manager. I'm tired of settling, period. I'm ready to start living my life."

And—silly or not—she'd begin with that list of ten things every woman should do. As soon as she'd seen it, she'd pulled out her Day-Timer and copied each item onto her Priority Action sheet. She'd start at the top and work her way down. And at the top of her list was Alex Moreno.

"Look, I've got to go," Jessica said.

"Just remember to sway your hips when you walk. And lick your lips a lot. And—"

"Patricia—"

"And…and, good luck!"

Jessica punched the off button and returned the phone to its cradle. Luck? She didn't need luck. She was a *Saucy* woman now. Or she would be soon. Once she checked all the items off The List.

STANDING ON THE doorstep of Jessica Sumners's quaint, ranch-style house, Alex Moreno felt as nervous as he had standing in her father's courtroom a decade ago.

Not for the first time since he'd moved back to Palo Verde, did he doubt his sanity. He'd moved home to prove to this town that he'd changed. That he wasn't the wild, reckless kid he'd been back in high school. He was now a successful businessman and upstanding member of the community. A damn paragon of responsibility.

All of which would have been a hell of a lot easier to prove if someone would actually hire him. He needed this job.

Despite that, he hated that his first job would be from her.

In the past decade he'd imagined seeing her again more often than he cared to admit. He'd pictured them meeting as equals, he casually mentioning the jobs he'd worked on in L.A. and the Bay Area, her suitably impressed by his success. Never once had he pictured standing on her doorstep, praying she'd hire him and thus resuscitate his dwindling bank balance.

As he rang the doorbell he caught a flash of movement through the leaded glass of her front door. His stomach turned over in anticipation.

Through the window, he saw her walk toward the door and swing it open. Her eyes flicked up the length of his body then came to rest on his face. Her smile faltered and he watched her struggle to keep it in place.

She looked nervous, but even nervous, she still took his

breath away. She wore a simple black dress, with her hair pulled back. A pearl hung from a silver chain around her neck. Her strained expression undermined the elegance of her appearance. Maybe she was dressed for a funeral. Either way, he saw a flicker of anxiety in her eyes. As if he was the cause of her heightened emotions.

"Alex." She murmured his name, almost caressing it with her mouth.

The sound of his name on her lips sent a wholly inappropriate shiver of pure lust through his gut.

Then she cleared her throat, swung the door open wide enough to let him in and held out her hand for his. "Thank you for coming on such short notice."

"No problem." Her hand felt small and warm, her handshake surprisingly firm. He pulled his hand from hers then held out the portfolio describing his experience and listing his references.

Jessica blinked in surprise at the folder, then finally took it. She barely glanced at it before laying it on the marble-topped table beside the door. Her gaze traveled down his length to settle somewhere near his feet.

"You wanted me to look at your kitchen," he reminded her. He'd come straight from work. His shoes, his clothes—hell, everything about him—carried the dust of a hundred construction sites. He worked for a living— hard, manual labor. That never bothered him…until this instant, standing on Jessica's doorstep.

"Oh, yes." She blushed, stepping aside so he could enter. "It's this way."

She gestured for him to follow her, then turned and walked through the wide doorway to the living room. Her hips swayed gently as she moved. The movement dragged his gaze down the long length of her legs to her bare feet.

Her little black dress did nothing for him…but, man, oh man, the sight of her bare feet twisted him into a few knots.

Her feet were narrow and delicate, but not tiny. The feet of a tall woman, with long, graceful toes and high arches. Pale…and perfect. Perfectly manicured. Perfectly buffed. The pampered feet of a rich woman.

He glanced down at his own dirt-crusted work boots.

She swiveled back toward him, one foot planted firmly on the ground, the other leg bent slightly at the knee, exposing the arch of her foot and accentuating the curve of her calf.

Between them stretched a good ten feet of pristine cream carpet. Carpet he would track dirt all over the second he crossed her threshold.

"It's through here." She pointed through the living room toward the west end of her house.

"Right." He wiped his feet on her doormat, but it didn't do much good. Giving up, he stepped through her doorway, excruciatingly aware of the dried mud that flaked off his boots onto her floor. Yep, some things never changed.

He'd aged ten years since he'd last seen Jessica Sumners. He'd traveled halfway across the country and back. He'd opened and run his own business. Built houses for people who could buy and sell the Sumners. But the second he'd stepped foot back in this town, he'd felt like a dirty *moja- dito*. Completely unworthy to even stand on her doorstep, let alone do or say any of the things he yearned to.

Jessica Sumners was the closest thing their little California town had to royalty. She came from a world of wealth and privilege, he, from one of dirt and sweat.

Not that Jess had ever treated him like a wetback. No, she'd treated him with the same cool but equable friendliness she'd treated everyone at their high school.

Except for a few short weeks in his senior year when their relationship had evolved into something more. Something he still couldn't define or explain. Something that still sometimes kept him up at night.

But based on her cool reception, he wasn't even sure she remembered those weeks. Either way, he'd be damned if he tracked dirt across the floor of the one person in this town who'd never treated him like filth. He reached down and tugged loose his laces, then toed off his boots. Grime ringed his white socks where his boots met his ankles, but there was nothing he could do about that.

He followed her into the kitchen, trying not to notice the seductive rhythm of her hips as she moved. Her long legs accentuated the length of her stride. No pretension or seduction there. Which made the pull even stronger.

"Well, this is it." She gestured broadly to the kitchen like a game-show hostess revealing the prize behind door number two.

Taking in the room, he frowned. White-painted cabinets, white appliances and dark green laminate countertops in a simple galley-style kitchen. Dated, but functional.

Scratching his chin, he asked, "What exactly were you looking to have done?"

She crept closer. Standing almost shoulder-to-shoulder, she studied the kitchen, head tilted slightly toward him. "I don't know." She shifted, her bare shoulder brushing his sleeve as she faced him. "I was hoping you'd have some ideas."

"On the phone you said you wanted to meet as soon as possible. You implied it was an emergency."

Her gaze shifted nervously away from his. She appraised the kitchen, her forehead furrowing in a frown, before saying, "Haven't you ever made a decision and wanted to act on it as soon as possible? Just wanted to get it over with?"

Those words, coming from any other rich white woman, would have irritated him. But somehow, coming from her, they didn't sound selfish or childish, but…frustrated. And very human.

They hinted at the girl he'd known all those years ago. Was the sensitive and kind girl still buried inside this gorgeous creature? The way his hope leaped at the idea made him chuckle.

Dang, but he was susceptible to her.

Her gaze snapped back to his. "You think that's funny?"

"No, I just…" His hasty reassurance caught in his throat. Her eyes—startlingly blue at this close range—were wide and vulnerable. "It was just unexpected."

She frowned. "In what way?"

"I don't know," he admitted. "Back in school you were always the perfect rich girl. The perfect student. I guess I never pictured you as the impatient type."

A hint of a smile tugged at her lips. "I'm surprised you bothered to picture me at all."

Oh, man, she had no idea. If she knew how many times and how many ways he'd pictured her back then, she wouldn't want him putting his hands anywhere near her kitchen. He could guaran-damn-tee it.

Keeping his mouth firmly shut on the subject, he said, "I'll tell you what—" He pulled his tape measure off his belt and his notepad out his back pocket. "I'll take some measurements, make some notes. We'll see what we can come up with."

Just holding the tape measure made him feel more at ease. Jessica may have money, but he had skills. He'd come a long way from the boy he'd been back in high school.

Moving from one end of the kitchen to the next, he measured the length and width, noting the depth and locations of each of the cabinets. He put his pad down on the countertop and began making a quick sketch of the kitchen as it was. She stood beside him, closer than was necessary, throwing off his concentration. And damn, she smelled so good he could barely think.

He shifted away from her, propping his hip against the countertop. "Are you willing to give up storage space? Maybe a wall?"

"What do you think?"

What did he think? He thought she was standing awfully close for someone who just wanted her kitchen remodeled.

Think about the money, he ordered himself. If she wanted to drop forty or fifty grand on a whim, he'd be happy to help her do it.

Think about *that*. Not about how she smells—fresh and clean, yet spicy. Like Ivory soap mixed with something decadent.

He cleared his throat. "If you're going to do it, do it right."

"So you think I should…"

"Knock out that wall." He pointed to the wall separating the kitchen from the living room. "You open up this space, the kitchen and the living room will feel bigger."

"Really? You can do that?"

"Sure." He crossed to the wall and rapped on the drywall beneath the upper cabinet. "We tear out this wall, put in a structural beam to support the ceiling and you've got a whole new kitchen. What'd you say?"

Come on, baby, take a bite. Just a little nibble.

She glanced at him, then back at the wall. Her eyes glazed over, just a little, as if she were trying to imagine what the room would look like. "It'd look great. I—"

She seemed to catch herself just short of saying yes. Shaking her head as if to clear it, she smiled shyly. "I should probably think about it first."

He'd almost had her. Then, bam, she was gone. Just like that.

Just his luck.

And if his luck didn't turn soon, he'd be flipping burgers down at the Dairy Barn. Work was scarce in Palo Verde. Scarce, if your name was Alex Moreno.

When he'd moved back here, he hadn't anticipated the animosity people in this town still harbored against him. But he was determined to prove he wasn't still the pain-in-the-ass kid he'd been back then. He'd do just about anything to prove it. He'd damn near beg if he had to.

"I'll tell you what… While you're thinking about it, I'll work up a few drawings. Give you an idea of what I'm picturing."

She looked unconvinced. And again it struck him as odd that she seemed so interested in him, yet so uninterested in her kitchen, when she'd been so insistent on the phone. If she'd been any other woman—anyone other than perfect Jessica Sumners—he'd have assumed she was hitting on him.

The Jessica he knew from high school was smart and fair and always treated people with dignity. And she absolutely did not invite guys she barely knew over to her house for a quick tussle in the sack.

She stepped even closer and placed her hand on his arm. She moistened her lips in a movement that somehow looked both outrageously sensuous and slightly embarrassed all at the same time. "Or maybe we could talk about it more over a drink." Her voice trembled and her hand felt surprisingly warm against his bare skin.

His gut clenched at her touch. He sucked in a deep breath and the air around him seemed laden with her scent.

Then her words hit him. A drink? She wanted to go out for a drink? Damn, she *was* hitting on him.

He jerked his arm away from her touch. "By 'go out for a drink,' do you mean, go out on a date?"

She shrugged, her shoulders shifting in a movement of graceful self-doubt. "I just thought…well, yes. I'd love to catch up with you. If you're interested."

He shook his head, laughing bitterly. Did he want to go out on a date with Jessica Sumners? Hell, yes.

But there was a gleam in her eyes that told him this wasn't just for old times' sake. How in God's name had he been so wrong about her?

One by one, the implications hit him square in the chest.

She'd asked him here to hit on him. Which meant she wasn't interested in hiring him. Which meant he wasn't going to get the job he desperately needed. Finally—and strangely, this was the blow that hurt the worst—she wasn't the sweet, open girl he remembered. She was, however, the kind of woman who liked to order in a little blue-collar fun for the afternoon.

The pisser was…he was tempted.

Staring down into her eyes, breathing in her scent, *and* the heat of her touch still burning his arm… Yeah, he was tempted. Jessica—rich, beautiful and damn near saintly in the eyes of this town—was hitting on him. If the look on her face was any indication, she wanted more from him than just a drink.

The temptation to give it to her, to toss his dignity out

the window, to pull her into his arms and explore that luscious mouth of hers almost overwhelmed him. Not just because she was beautiful, but also because kissing
Jessica…hell, pulling off her expensive dress and nailing
her right here in her kitchen…would be the ultimate teenage fantasy brought to life. Making it with the most beautiful, well-respected girl in town. The girl he'd wanted so
bad it had made his teeth ache.

The temptation was too strong. Finally giving in to what
he'd wanted ever since walking through that front door—
hell, to what he'd wanted all his life—he reached out and
ran his fingertips down her cheek to her jawline and
nudged her chin up. His thumb brushed against her moist
lower lip, tugging it open.

"Is this what you want?" he asked. He inched closer to
her, a little surprised when she actually swayed toward
him, instead of shying away.

"Yes."

Her bare knee brushed against his jeans, her foot
nudged his. He glanced down. The simple intimacy of the
touch, her bare foot against his sock, struck him. Her perfect, pampered foot nuzzled up against his dirty work sock.

He dropped his hand from her face and stepped back,
angry with himself for wanting what he couldn't have.
And with her for making him want it.

"That's why you called me, isn't it? That's why you
needed me to come over right away?"

She blinked, her eyes wide with surprise, and maybe
confusion. "No." Her no wasn't forceful enough to convince even herself. "Maybe."

"You don't really want to have your kitchen remodeled, do you?"

Her gaze shifted nervously from his. "No. I just…" She

took in a noticeably shaky breath and pressed her palm to the countertop as if she needed something to hold her up. "I just thought…"

"What? That it would be fun to jump in the sack with the manual laborer?"

"No!" Her spine stiffened.

"Then what?"

"It's complicated," she insisted, her voice now firm. "This was obviously a mistake."

"Right. Obviously." He ripped the top page out of his notepad and crumpled it into a ball. "Did it ever occur to you that this is my job? This is how I make my living?"

She arched one perfect eyebrow. "Did it ever occur to you that I might honestly have wanted just a date? That not every woman wants to jump in the sack with you?"

If he hadn't been so angry, he might have laughed at her bravado. From the way her voice stumbled, he'd be willing to bet good money she'd never used the phrase "jump in the sack" before in her life.

"Not interested, huh?" Before she could protest, he wrapped his hands around her arms, pulled her to him and kissed her.

He told himself he was doing it to prove a point.

But the second he felt her body against his, he knew he'd lied. The only point he wanted to prove was that she was as kissable as she looked. Man, was she ever.

Her lips were warm and smooth beneath his. She tasted like red wine, which surprised him, because he would have sworn she was the kind of woman who drank white wine.

When her tongue darted out to brush against his lips, surprise was the least of his reactions. Hot, aching desire hit him hard in the gut.

Abruptly he pushed her away. She looked as shell-shocked as he felt. She pressed her fingertips to her mouth, glaring at him.

"That was rude," she finally said.

He laughed out loud, gathering up his notepad and measuring tape before heading for the door. "It's rude to kiss someone who's clearly asking for it, but not rude to interrupt the middle of someone's workday and waste their time?"

She trotted after him. "I didn't think you would mind. I—"

He spun back around to face her. "Well, I do. Apparently you have nothing better to do on a Friday afternoon but jerk people around. But I've got work to do." She flinched as if stung by his criticism, but he didn't stop. As he shoved first one foot and then the other into his boots and tugged them on, he continued. "Real work, princess. Not imaginary work that bored debutantes make up because they want a playmate. Work I'll get paid for."

"You don't think *I* work?"

Shaking his head at her indignation—*her* indignation!—he snapped, "I don't care whether or not you work. I don't care if you're bored or lonely or horny or whatever it is that made you decide you wanted someone to come over and play. I care that you're wasting my time. Goodbye, princess."

AND WITH THAT, he was gone. The door slammed behind him hard enough to actually rattle the windows.

For a second she stood there, fuming at the closed door and shooting angry glares around the empty foyer. Then she propped her hands on her hips and said—to no one in particular, "You are the last man I'd invite to come over and play, even if I was bored or lonely or—" she sputtered, then forced herself to say the word "—horny. Which I am not."

Except she was.

It was as if her body had come alive again at Alex's touch. And as if it had gone through electric shock treatments at his kiss.

She felt hot and tingly. Exposed.

She spun on her heel and stomped to the kitchen where she poured herself another glass of wine. She sipped it slowly, making sure she was perfectly calm before taking the last sip. Then she carefully poured herself some more, even though what she really wanted to do was to throw the goblet to the floor.

Halfway through the glass, she set the crystal aside, propped her elbows on the countertop and buried her head in her hands.

How in the world had that gone so wrong?

How had she so drastically underestimated how she'd respond to him? She'd just wanted to see him again. To size up his potential as a "Passionate Fling-ee." Instead he'd made her all googly-eyed and she'd practically attacked him. No wonder he'd gotten the wrong impression.

He was a different person than he'd been in high school. Taller, for one thing. And he'd lost some of his wiry thinness. Now, he was lean, but muscular. Powerful. And so handsome, it made her ache.

One thing was sure. Seeing him answered the question of whether or not he still got to her. From the moment she'd opened the door, she'd felt his pull deep in her gut.

When he'd asked her what she'd wanted, her mind had just gone blank. She'd wanted him. Some part of her had always wanted him.

And now he'd probably never talk to her again, which was going to make apologizing very difficult.

She straightened and turned around. Propping her back against the counter, she reached for her glass of wine. From the corner of her eye, she saw the crumpled ball of paper Alex had tossed aside.

She picked it up then flattened it with her hand to work out the wrinkles. There was a black-ink sketch of her kitchen, surprisingly accurate, with measurements written on the side in Alex's masculine handwriting.

The seriousness with which he'd approached the project only humiliated her. Shaking her head at her own stupidity, she carefully folded the note in quarters.

Yep, she owed Alex an apology. And if she knew him half as well as she thought she did—

No, scratch that. She clearly didn't know him at all. But she suspected he wasn't going to make it easy on her.

She crossed to where her Day-Timer sat propped in one of the kitchen chairs and opened it to her Priority Action sheet. There was The List.

1. Find Your Fling.
2. Don't Be a Homebody.
3. Go Tribal.
4. Release Your Inner Dominatrix.
5. Be a Diva in Bed.
6. Drop the Drawers.
7. Live in the Fast Lane.
8. Just Admit It.
9. Shake Up Your Space.
10. Conquer It.

Number one—Find Your Fling—taunted her. How could she have a passionate fling without Alex, when he was the one man she felt passionately about?

Then she scanned down to number eight: Just Admit It. "Own up to a big mistake."

Well, it looked as though she'd soon be able to cross one of the items off The List after all.

2

THE THOUGHT OF SEEING Alex again made Jessica's stomach twist into nervous knots.

At least, that's what she told herself. Those knots in her stomach were knots of dread, not excitement. And the jittery feeling she got at the thought of seeing him again had nothing to do with the way he'd kissed her. The way his roughened palms had made the bare skin of her arms tingle. The way he'd smelled unlike any other man she'd ever known—an appealing mix of sunshine, dust and sweat.

She blew out a long, slow breath.

Yep. Just nerves. That was it.

She'd armed herself with his business card and an outfit less likely to attract snide "princess" comments—black capri pants and a black, boat-necked T-shirt. It was as good an outfit as any to grovel in.

According to the card she'd salvaged from the portfolio he'd given her, Moreno Construction operated out of his home, which turned out to be a small bungalow-style house on the outskirts of town. Finding the house was not nearly as difficult as finding the courage to walk up the overgrown path to the door. But, she conceded, owning up to mistakes was not supposed to be easy.

She rang the doorbell, waited a full minute then rang it

again. The front door was open, and through the screen door, she caught glimpses of the darkened interior. But no sign of Alex himself.

Then from deep within, she heard a male voice shout, "Come in."

She opened the screen door, stepped over the threshold and closed the door behind her. The entry opened straight into the living room, which ran the width of the house. A collection of standard-issue bachelor furniture sat clumped in the center of the room. Moving boxes flanked the walls in stacks three or four high. From where she stood, she caught a clear view of the dining room and the kitchen beyond. More bland furniture, more boxes. Only the kitchen looked lived in, with a couple of cereal bowls on the counter and a pizza box wedged into a trash can.

From somewhere at the back of the house, a power tool roared to life, so she followed the sound down the hall to a back bedroom.

And sure enough, there was Alex. He stood on an A-frame ladder, straddling the peak. The stance accentuated the muscles of his long legs. With one hand, he held up a sheet of drywall, with the other, he used a cordless drill to drive screws into the sheet.

With the exception of the spot where Alex worked, the walls had been stripped down to the studs. Chalky dust from the drywall hung in the air, making her cough.

He turned at the sound and stared at her for a second. Disbelief and then suspicion registered in his eyes before he turned back to the drywall and drove in three more screws.

Watching him move, Jessica found herself fascinated by the way his broad shoulders shifted under the threadbare cotton of his white T-shirt. By the hole in his jeans that bared his knee and the worn patches of denim along the length of his thighs and down his zipper.

She was used to seeing men dressed in Dockers and button-down Oxford shirts. Three-piece suits and tuxedoes. Clothes designed to advertise a man's wealth and social position. Funny how none of those clothes spoke of a man's strength—a man's ability to work with his hands—the way Alex's worn jeans and grimy T-shirt did.

Funny how she now noticed how appealing those qualities were. How they made her skin tingle with excitement.

When he swung one leg over the peak of the ladder and climbed down, she averted her eyes, trying not to gawk. After all, he'd made it clear he just wasn't interested. As he nodded in greeting, he dusted off his hands, then wedged them into his back pockets. Not the warmest reception, but about the best she could hope for under the circumstances.

"I wanted to apologize for yesterday. And to explain."

At her words, the suspicion in his gaze seemed to flicker and go out, but his eyes were dark and mysterious regardless, so she couldn't be sure.

Stepping to her side, he stopped just short of touching her and instead gestured toward the door.

"It'll be less dusty outside."

As with most houses in Palo Verde, the backyard sloped away from the house, up toward the foothills. A patch of overgrown fruit trees lined the far fence and crowded against the detached garage. A picnic table sat proudly in the center of a lawn of close-cropped weeds. It was a far cry from her own neatly manicured, obsessively maintained backyard.

When she turned her gaze to Alex, she found him

watching her carefully, as if gauging her reaction. Once again she found his inscrutable dark gaze unsettling.

"It's nice," she said, carefully lowering herself to the bench seat of the picnic table.

He stared at her in blank disbelief.

"Come fall, you'll really enjoy the apples from those trees."

"My parents have worked in the apple orchards for over thirty years. I hate apples," he said flatly as he sat opposite her.

Wow. Could this go any worse?

He crossed his arms over his chest and eyed her speculatively. And though she felt her pulse leap at his perusal, there was little flattering in his expression. "So, did you come here to talk about my landscaping or did you just think it'd be fun to waste another of my afternoons?"

Just when she was starting to hope someone would come by and shoot her with a tranquilizer gun just to put her out of her misery, she noticed his lips twitching.

He was enjoying this. Not out of cruelty, she was fairly certain, but he seemed to like having her at a disadvantage. That should have annoyed her, but it didn't. Something in his smile short-circuited her synapses. "As I said, I came here to apologize," she said again, trying to be blunt. Get this over with as quickly as possible. After all, he may enjoy flustering her, but she didn't enjoy being flustered. "I think you got the wrong impression yesterday."

He arched an eyebrow in speculation. "You mean you *do* want me to remodel your kitchen?"

"No. But you seemed to think I invited you over just to…sleep with you. But that's not why I called you."

"So you don't want to sleep with me?"

"No!" A second too late, she saw the teasing glint in his gaze. He was toying with her.

"You'll think it's stupid."

"Tell me anyway," he coaxed.

And, oddly enough, she wanted to. It'd been like that when they were in school, too. Something about Alex Moreno made her believe she could trust him implicitly. That she could tell him anything. And he'd never hurt her. Of course, it didn't help matters that he seemed so much less angry than he had yesterday. Even less than he had when she'd arrived. Her apology had gone a long way toward softening him up. Score one for *Saucy* magazine.

"It all started with this list." No, that wasn't right. "Actually it all started with my trip to Sweden."

"Sweden?" he asked, his mouth set in an inexplicably grim line.

"For business. I write software for PalmPilots. Companies hire us to write programs for them. Software that tracks sales, shipping, delivery, that kind of thing. So I went to Sweden to install it and train them to use it. I went with the understanding that when I came home, I'd have this big promotion."

"Let me guess. You didn't get the promotion."

"Three days before I came home, they gave it to someone else. You know the really ironic thing? The whole time I was in Sweden, everyone kept talking about how hard I worked. That I did the work of three people. Everyone was amazed. But you know what? I didn't work any harder there than I do here. But that's when I saw The List."

"'The List'?"

"In a magazine I was reading on the flight home. '10 Things Every Woman Should Do.' I decided right then and there that I was going to do everything on that list. I know it sounds silly, thinking that some list from a mag- azine will change your life, but I'm tired of settling for doing the work without the recognition. I'm tired of put- ting my life on hold while I wait for some promotion that may never come."

She studied his face, looking for some sign that he found this as silly as she did, now that she heard herself saying it out loud. But his expression was carefully blank, so she said with a shrug, "I know it's just a list, but it's a start."

"So how do I fit into all this? What exactly is on this list that you think I can help you do?"

The question she'd been dreading. But he certainly de- served her honesty, if nothing else. She swallowed hard, embarrassment burning her cheeks. The idea of discuss- ing sex with Alex made other less visible parts of her burn, as well. "Number one on the list is 'Find Your Fling.'"

He nodded and for a second she thought he wasn't going to respond, but then he asked, "And you thought I'd be a good candidate?"

She shrugged, wishing desperately he wasn't so blasé about this whole thing, as if women propositioned him all the time. Though, for all she knew, they did. For all she knew, she was just one in a long line of lonely women who wanted to have a passionate fling with Alex.

And if that was the case, no wonder he'd been so an- noyed with her yesterday. Of course, she still hadn't owned up to her mistake, not completely. So she sucked in a deep breath and said, "Yes, I thought you'd be a good candidate. And not because I wanted to fool around with the hired help."

Something in his eyes caught and held her attention. Once again she felt the gut-level tug of attraction. Passion, yes. But something more. Something more unsettling than that.

She waited a moment, hoping he'd say something. When he didn't, she moved to leave. "I should go."

But he grabbed her arm to stop her. "Wait—"

For a moment they simply sat there, his palm warm against her arm, the delicate skin at the crook of her elbow sensitized to the touch of his work-roughened fingers.

In that instant she knew—she hadn't come here to apologize. She didn't want him to forgive her. She'd come here hoping... Hoping what?

That he wanted her as much as she wanted him?

That the kiss they'd shared yesterday had been more than just a kiss?

That it had kept him up all night—hot and wanting— as it had her?

Yes, yes and yes. What she'd really wanted was for him to touch her again. After a lifetime of being coddled and cosseted by men with soft hands, she wanted this rough man—these hands—to touch her. Just once she wanted to know how that felt.

Too bad he didn't seem to want the same thing.

Okay, maybe he was a little interested. After all, that kiss in the kitchen had been pretty hot. But she wanted more. She wanted the kind of passion he couldn't walk away from.

She never again wanted to settle for less than that.

ALEX WATCHED HER as she scooted off the bench and stood. She made it about three steps down the driveway toward her car before he stopped her. He didn't know why, but he didn't want her to leave like this.

"Wait, Jessica."

She swung back to face him, her spine unnaturally stiff, her chin a notch higher. Outwardly she seemed so together. Cool and in control. But there was vulnerability there, too. *That* was what he couldn't walk away from.

"Why me? When you decided you wanted to have a passionate fling, why'd you pick me?"

He was an idiot for asking. But he wanted to spend more time with her almost as much as he wanted to take her to bed and do all kinds of sinful things to her body.

Jessica didn't answer right away. For a long moment she just studied him, her head tilted at an angle that let a lock of her hair fall across her cheek. Her expression was cautious, as if she were trying to decide whether or not to tell him the truth.

Finally she said, "I had a crush on you in high school. I was a junior, and you were a senior. It all started one day when—" Her gaze darted away from his and the barest hint of a blush crept into her cheeks. "You probably don't even remember it."

"Try me."

But he did remember. He knew exactly which day she meant.

"I was walking home from school alone one day. A couple of boys cornered me by the old Dawson house, where I used to cut across the creek. One of them was that Morse boy. Ronald, I think. His brother had been picked up for drunk driving. This was back when my father was still a judge and he'd just sentenced Ronald's brother. He was a repeat offender. My father had no choice. But Ronald was looking for someone to blame. I guess I was an easy target."

The way she said it—so simply, with no resentment or anger in her voice—made him wonder how often that kind of thing had happened. How many of her fellow students had resented her, hated her even, because of the power her father yielded?

"So there I was, all alone with these three guys, when you came along and—"

"Saved you." He finished the sentence for her because he couldn't stand to hear the hero worship in her voice.

Her gaze snapped back to his. "You do remember."

As if it were yesterday. In vivid detail. And he remembered all the things she was leaving out and skimming over. Her "a couple of boys" had been three huge guys. Football players, if he remembered right. Big, dumb and just looking for an excuse to pin Jessica Sumners up against a tree.

Which was exactly where they'd had her when he'd come along. She must have been terrified, but there hadn't even been a glimmer of emotion in her eyes. She hadn't begged or cried out or even fought them, as if she'd instinctively known that would only incite their rage. Instead she'd stood there, her gaze as calm and steady as her voice as she'd talked to Ronald.

Her tone so soft, Alex hadn't caught much of what she'd said. Something about how this would be for the best. How his brother could get the help he needed.

Alex had stood there, half hidden by the fence, his blood pounding, waiting to see what would happen. Unable to leave her to fend for herself, if the guys didn't walk away, he'd have to do something. But jeez, they were huge. And he'd been in enough fights to know he hadn't stood a chance, not against all three.

"It all happened so fast," she mused. "One minute I was all alone, the next I was surrounded." She looked up now, her eyes finding his. "And then you were there."

When he'd seen Morse lean in toward her, he'd acted instinctively. He'd called out her name. Not Jessica. Not Sumners, which was what Morse had been calling her. But "Jess."

"You called out to me," she said, still studying him with that pensive expression that made him so uncomfortable. "It must have surprised them, because they all three turned around and I was able to get away."

She'd run straight to his side. Without thinking, he'd put his arm around her shoulder. Together, they'd walked through the Dawson's yard to the street. At the sidewalk, he'd dropped his arm, but kept walking beside her, not wanting to let her out of his sight. Especially when he'd glanced over his shoulder to see all three guys standing in front of the Dawson house, watching them.

After they'd turned the corner and were out of sight of the football players, she'd slipped her hand into his. He'd felt her palm damp against his and her fingers trembling, and only then had he known how scared she'd been.

When they'd reached her block, he'd stopped and tried to pull his hand away, but she'd held tight. All he could think at the time was that he'd never imagined he'd ever find himself holding Jessica Sumners's hand. And he sure as hell had never imagined it would feel that good.

Then she'd looked up at him, her eyes bluer than any he'd ever seen, her expression so serious. Not distant and reserved, as it had been the few times their eyes had met while passing in the halls, but warm and filled with emotion. Gratitude, sure, but something else, as well.

An awareness of him. As if she was seeing him for the very first time. Hell, maybe she was. Girls like Jessica— good girls—didn't notice him. And for all he knew, she'd never really looked at him until that moment.

She'd stood so close to him that when the breeze picked up, a long strand of her hair fluttered close to his face and he'd caught the scent of her. She'd even smelled rich. Clean and fresh. Not like strong perfume, the way his sisters did.

In that instant he'd been distinctly aware of two things. First, he'd wanted to kiss her. Desperately. He'd wanted to press his lips to hers to see if she tasted as rich as she smelled.

Second, he shouldn't even be touching her.

Jessica Sumners was perfect. She never got into trouble, she never got her hands dirty, and she sure as hell never kissed guys like him. Not in darkened cars late at night when no one could see her and certainly not in the middle of the day forty feet from her front door.

Less than a month before, he had stood in her father's courtroom and been ordered by Judge Sumners to "keep his nose clean and stay out of trouble."

He'd suspected making out with the judge's daughter would get him into a great deal of trouble.

Despite that—or maybe because of it—he'd pulled his hand from hers and shoved it into his pocket. It had been one of the hardest things he'd ever done.

When she'd opened her mouth to say something, he'd interrupted her. "I'll stay here and watch until you're inside." She'd nodded. "Don't walk home alone again. Wait to walk home in a group. The bigger the better."

"I'll have our maid pick me up at school until this blows over."

Of course. Her maid. Why hadn't he thought of that? "Good idea."

She'd seemed to want to say something else as she'd watched him with those huge blue eyes. Eyes that seemed full of something perilously close to hero worship. Hell, that had been the last thing he'd needed. Jessica Sumners getting a crush on him.

Damn, that'd screw up his life but good.

"Go on." He'd nodded toward her house. Keeping his tone bored, he'd added, "I got things to do."

Her gaze had flickered as she'd turned and hurried toward the imposing mansion. She hadn't looked back. Hadn't seen that he'd stood on the corner, watching her house for nearly thirty minutes, belying his comment about having things to do.

Now, all these years later, as Jessica stood in his driveway, he thought again about how nothing had changed. She was as out of his reach now as she had been on that long-ago spring afternoon. And she still seemed unaware of how much he wanted her.

"I looked for you the next day at school," she said. "I guess I wanted—" She shrugged. "I don't know."

She may not have known what she'd wanted all those years ago, but he had. She'd wanted to recapture that connection they'd both felt standing on that street corner, her hand in his and the rush of adrenaline still pounding through their veins.

She looked at him now, her expression unguarded. When she looked at him like that, he felt like a hero. Ironic, given the very unheroic things his libido was urging him to do.

"So that's why you came to me? Because I saved you from some bullies?"

She frowned, looking very unsure of herself. "Not exactly."

"Then what?" When she didn't answer, he leaned forward. "I didn't do anything anyone else wouldn't have done."

Now her eyes met his with a flash of annoyance. As if it irritated her to hear him belittle his actions.

He sighed. "Look, Jess, it sounds to me like all these years you've been walking around thinking I'm some kind of a hero. But that's just not true. I didn't rescue you. I wasn't a hero. To tell the truth, I wasn't even a very nice guy."

"I don't believe you," she snapped. "What you did might not have meant anything to you, but it did to me."

"A momentary lapse in judgment."

Shaking her head, she exhaled loudly. "Would it really be so bad?"

"What?"

"Would it really be so bad to let people know that under your rebellious, tough-guy exterior, deep down inside you're actually a nice, decent human being?"

His heart swelled at her words—but it only reminded him of another body part that tended to swell around her. Not sure how much more hero worship he could take, he purposely lightened the mood.

He reached over and chucked her gently on the chin. "That's where you're wrong, Jess. Deep down inside, I'm just like I am on the outside."

She stiffened. "I don't believe you. You wanted people to think you're despicable, but you weren't."

"Despicable?" He laughed. "Honey, villains with big mustaches in old silent movies are despicable."

The irritation flashed in her eyes again but quickly disappeared. However, it wasn't as easy to hide the blush his teasing had brought to her cheeks. She pressed her lips into a thin line. "Okay. So not despicable."

Sensing he was close to having her exactly where he wanted her, he pressed his advantage. "No. Not despicable." And because he just couldn't resist touching her, he reached for her hand. Instead of taking it in his, he flipped it over, exposing her palm to his touch. "I'm much worse than despicable. You know what I was thinking about the whole way home?" She shook her head. "I was thinking about how I wanted to kiss you."

"But—"

He didn't let her finish. "There you were thinking I was some kind of a hero and all I could think about was how to get in your pants." He didn't look at her, didn't take his eyes away from her palm, which he couldn't seem to stop touching. It was so incredibly soft and warm under his fingertips. "I would have nailed you in a minute if you'd given me the chance."

She pulled her hand away. "I don't believe you."

This time he couldn't stop himself from meeting her gaze. He studied her face, but for once found it almost impossible to read her expression.

"As you pointed out," she said. "There I was, thinking you were a hero. If all you'd wanted was to—"

When she hesitated, he supplied the words for her. "Nail you."

She nodded. "If that was really what you wanted from me, you could have had it then."

At her near-whispered words, blood surged through his groin, nearly destroying the last of his control. But her calm and steady gaze assured him of her seriousness. He laughed ruefully. "It's probably a good thing I didn't know that then."

Now she was the one to laugh, clearly embarrassed. "And here all this time, I assumed you did know and just weren't interested." He shot her a questioning look and she shrugged sheepishly. "I looked for you all that next week at school, but every time I saw you, you were with friends. Or that girlfriend of yours. What was her name?"

Alex had to search his memory. Funny, he'd dated "that girlfriend of his" for months, but he could barely remember her name, let alone picture her. Yet he still remembered the expression on Jessica's face when she'd put her hand into his. And the color of the shirt she'd been wearing. And the way she'd smelled. And—

"Sandra," he finally supplied.

"Right. Sandra. Every time I saw you that week, you were with her. At first, I thought you were avoiding me on purpose."

"I was. It wouldn't have been in either of our best interests if people thought there was something going on between us."

He'd known even then how impossible a relationship with her would be. Even a friendship would have caused problems. She was the a straight-A student and the daughter of the county judge. He was the son of a migrant farm worker, already a grade behind in school, in and out of more trouble than she could imagine, his police record already burgeoning. None of that had kept him from wanting her, but it had damn well kept him from acting on it.

He'd avoided her so effectively that she'd eventually resorted to slipping a note in his locker. Three simple lines thanking him for coming to her rescue, in neat, cursive writing on pale pink paper.

"I thought that you knew I'd developed a crush on you and were trying to discourage me," she said now.

"I was."

Her gaze darted to his, her eyes a vivid blue that he seemed to have no defenses against. "Then why did you write me back?"

Because he'd just plain been unable to resist.

He shrugged. "I don't know."

His response, slipped through the vent of her locker during fifth period, had started a flurry of notes. She wrote him every day, often more than once, about things both wonderful and absurdly out of the realm of his experience—a low score on a chemistry exam, the shoes her mother had had dyed to match for some party dress, the fight she'd had with her parents over whether or not she'd go to tennis camp over the summer.

He'd written her less often, but with almost unbearable attention to detail. He'd penned his notes to her in the library, hunched over the dictionary, carefully checking his spelling, scouring the thesaurus for words he thought would make him look smart. Words like "supposition" and "eradicate."

Those three weeks that they'd exchanged notes had been some of the happiest of his young life. Then one day he'd received a note from her asking if he wanted to take her to the prom.

He'd known he couldn't do it, but God how he'd wanted to. And he hadn't had the heart to say no. So he'd just stopped writing to her.

"I know you thought I was just some annoying kid," she said now. "But I loved getting those notes from you. I'd pretend, just for a little while, that I was your girlfriend, instead of Sandra." She paused for a heartbeat, lost in some long-ago memory. "It was like you couldn't keep your hands off her. Did you know, I even saw you kissing her once?"

He did know. He remembered the moment vividly. He'd been avoiding Jessica all week, but she hadn't taken the hint when he'd stopped answering her notes. Every time he'd turned around, there she'd be. His patience and his willpower had started to wear thin. She hadn't ever caught him alone, but he'd been sure she eventually would. He'd been sure she'd look up at him with those impossibly blue eyes and that when she did he wouldn't be able to resist doing something incredibly stupid, like kiss her.

So he'd done something he was sure would scare her

off. He'd kissed Sandra in front of her. Not an innocent little peck on the mouth, either, but a full-bodied, open-
mouthed, I-can't-wait-to-get-your-body-naked kiss.

"I'd never seen anyone kiss like that," Jessica admitted
with a little laugh. "Not in real life anyway. That kiss…it
was like something out of movie. And I remember thinking, 'So that's passion.' I'd never been kissed like that." She
laughed nervously, the pink returning to her cheeks. "I still
haven't."

"Jess—"

Her hands were clasped tightly together and she was
staring pointedly down at them. "All my life and I've
never been kissed like that. Never felt that kind of passion.
Or had anyone feel that kind of passion about me."

The sheer yearning in her voice finally wore him down
and he reached out and put his hand over hers. "Jess," he
said again.

This time she looked up at him. Her eyes held none of
the emotion he'd expected to see. Just a glimmer of resignation. Nothing more.

But she pulled her hand out from under his. Then she
turned, hitching her purse strap up on her shoulder as she
made to leave. "Don't feel sorry for me."

"I don't," he protested. "But if you think no man's ever
felt passion for you, I think you may be seriously under-
estimating the effect you have on men."

Her gaze narrowed and she shook her head dismissively. "I don't need your pity. And I certainly don't need
you to massage my ego. I only brought it up because I
didn't want you to think that yesterday was just—what was
that phrase you used?— me wanting to screw around with
the hired help. I don't think of you that way. I never have."

She continued down his driveway toward the street,

but only made it a few feet before he stopped her. "Then what was it?"

"I guess I just wanted someone to feel that kind of passion for me." This time, when she turned to leave, he just let her go.

Because if she stayed any longer, he might break down and tell her the truth. That he did feel that way about her. That he'd wanted her badly even back then. That, apparently, he still wanted her now.

And that she *had* inspired the kind of passion she'd spoken of.

That day back in high school, when she'd seen him kiss Sandra, it wasn't Sandra he'd been kissing. Oh, it had been Sandra's body pressed to his and Sandra's mouth under his lips. But when he'd closed his eyes, it had been Jessica's face he'd seen. And Jessica's scent he'd smelled. It had been Jessica he'd wanted to kiss.

He'd known then he couldn't have her, but that hadn't kept him from wanting her. And it didn't now.

3

"So WHAT YOU and I need to do," Patricia said as she pulled Jessica through her front door a week later, "is find you another man to have a wild fling with."

As she was dragged toward Patricia's bedroom, Jessica tried to protest. "I don't want to find another guy."

Patricia paused to prop her hands on her hips like a drill sergeant. "You want to do all the things on The List, don't you?"

"Yes, but—"

"There's no 'yes, but' about it. If you want to complete the list, you need another guy. Which is why you and I are going clubbing."

"Clubbing?" She narrowed her gaze suspiciously. "I thought you said we were just going to hang out."

"We *are* just going to hang out. At a club."

"Do we have to?"

"Yes, we have to. If we don't go out, you can't meet men." Patricia ticked off her points on her fingers as she spoke. "If you don't meet men, you'll never be able to do all the things on that list." Her voice dropped to a low growl. "You're not giving up on The List are you? Are you?"

Feeling even more like a young recruit at boot camp, Jessica snapped to attention. "Sir, no, sir!"

Patricia eyed her shrewdly for a second before cracking a smile. "That's more like it." She clapped her hands together. "Now we just have to find something for you to wear."

Jessica looked down at her clothes. "I can't wear this?"

"Um…no. You look like you're going to an English tea party."

"But—"

"Trust me when I tell you that where we're going, you'll look out of place." With that, Patricia disappeared into her closet. A few minutes later she peered around the door. "Do you trust me?"

Uh, oh. This didn't sound good.

Jessica hesitated, but then she thought of The List and nodded firmly. "I trust you."

"Great!" Patricia emerged, her arms laden with clothes, the fingers of one hand clutching a pair of knee-high, black patent-leather boots. They looked like something a superhero would wear along with a bright red spandex outfit.

Jessica eyed the boots warily. "Seriously?"

"You trust me, right?" Patricia's lips curved in a mischievous smile. "You said you did."

"Maybe."

"The boots go with the outfit." Patricia tossed the boots onto the bed and began sorting through the clothes. "You're not weird about wearing other people's shoes, are you?"

Other people's shoes? Maybe a little weird. Other people's superhero boots? That was a whole 'nother bag of Skittles.

"I'm not sure we wear the same size," she pointed out.

Patricia planted her foot on the floor beside Jessica's. "Close enough. Besides, they're big on me. They should be perfect on you."

Eyeing the boots with trepidation, she murmured, "Great."

Patricia snorted with laughter. "Here, put this on."

She tossed a tank top at Jessica, who caught it automatically then let it dangle by the straps from her fingers. "This? You want me to wear this?" She was a good four inches taller than Patricia. "This won't fit me."

"Yes, it will. It's stretchy."

"That's not reassuring."

Next, she tossed Jessica a skirt. A very tiny skirt.

"No. No way."

"You said you trusted me."

"I lied."

"You'll look hot. Besides, it's leather."

"So?"

"Wasn't one of the things on The List something about wearing leather?"

Yes, but Jessica chose to ignore the question. "I can't wear this. I'll look ridiculous."

Patricia thrust out her hand in a I-don't-want-to-hear-it gesture. "When was the last time you went to a club?"

"Last weekend."

"Not the country club. An actual club."

"College," she admitted.

"Okay, so you haven't been to a club in ten years—"

"Seven."

"Whatever." Patricia waved her hand in exasperation, then rolled her eyes, in case the hand-waving wasn't enough. "Think about why you're doing the things on this list. You don't want to settle for being plain, boring ol' Jessica Sumners anymore, right? You want to be saucy. Like the magazine. Then be *Saucy*."

"Okay. Be *Saucy*," she repeated resolutely as she tugged on the clothes. The tank top fit better than she would have thought. The neck draped loosely, skimming the tops of her breasts. The hem just reached the low-slung skirt, teasing but not revealing.

She picked up one of the boots and studied it speculatively. "With a miniskirt? Really?"

"You'll look hot."

Still doubtful, but determined to be saucy, she tugged on the boots before standing and looking down at her outfit. The skirt was a good ten inches shorter than anything she'd ever worn. The tank top exposed glimpses of her midriff every time she moved. And the boots... Well, let's just say, if her mother ever saw her wearing them, she'd faint dead away into her martini glass.

Patricia sighed. "Alex would be on his knees begging if he could see you now."

"That would be nice," she said with a chuckle.

Patricia came to stand beside her. Shoulder to shoulder, they stared at their reflections in the mirror.

"Well, forget about Alex," Patricia said. "You look so good you'll have to pry men off you with a paint scraper! And I say, we don't leave that club alone. We'll definitely find you the perfect guy for your fling."

Despite Patricia's bravado, Jessica had her doubts. What she wanted was someone who would:

A. Drop everything to have a wild passionate fling with her.
B. Want her so passionately, he forgot everything but her. And,
C. Make her forget all about Alex.

Yep, that about summed it up. In other words, she wanted a freakin' miracle. She didn't need superhero boots, she needed Dorothy's red shoes.

ALEX HAD NEVER BEEN one to find redemption at the bottom of a bottle. Then again—he mused as he tipped the longneck back—he'd never really looked for it there.

He emptied the beer then set it down on the faux wood tabletop. The condensation and the slight tilt of the uneven table legs pulled the bottle closer to the edge, but his brother, Tomas, grabbed it before it could crash to the floor.

The table—like the rest of the decor—was a little too slick for his taste. Music blasted from the bar's sound system and a mile-long row of bottles lined the mirrored wall on the other side of the gleaming, polished bar. This wasn't a real bar, it was bar lite. Purified for the yuppies. But Tomas was buying and it was Alex's first night out since he'd arrived back in town. Who was he to complain?

"What do you think?" Tomas gestured at the room with his beer.

Alex hid his smile and his sarcastic comment. "It's great. You come here often?"

Tomas took a sip from his bottle, but couldn't hide his own mischievous smile. "Never been here before. I think it's absolute crap. But thanks for lying."

"If you think it's crap, why'd you bring me?"

"You seemed like you needed to blow off a little steam."

Even as he protested, he knew Tomas was right. He appreciated his brother's efforts, but he wasn't sure how much good it would do. The bar was little more than a pickup joint catering to Palo Verde's growing yuppie population. The beautiful women were plentiful and scantily clad. And if he'd been interested, he probably could've snagged one.

But, right now, the only woman he wanted to take to bed was Jessica Sumners.

He told himself she was all wrong for him. They had

nothing in common. Sleeping with her would get him nothing but a few moments' pleasure. None of that mattered. None of that had driven her from his thoughts.

And—so far—neither had the beer he'd been drinking.

He picked up the empty bottle. "You want another one?"

Tomas nodded. "Sure."

A few minutes later he was working his way back through the crowd, holding a pair of longnecks, when Jessica walked in. The way she was dressed, he almost didn't recognize her, but her posture gave her away. Even in a bar, she had the bearing of a princess. The sight of her jerked him to a standstill.

She was with a friend...someone shorter and curvier with platinum-blond hair. Beside her friend, Jessica looked like a goddess—one of those water sprite things he'd read about in school, tall and willowy. Her honey-blond hair tumbled over her shoulder in gleaming waves. Her eyes widened and shifted nervously as she glanced around the room.

Then, almost as if she sensed him watching her, her gaze drifted to his. She took half a step back and bumped into the door behind her. Her eyes darted from his as she frowned and tugged on her shirt.

The action called his gaze to her clothes and his hands clenched the necks of the beer bottles. Her outfit was no more revealing than the clothes of any other woman in the bar and less so than many. Neither her clothes nor the gorgeous body underneath held his attention—though the combination packed a powerful punch. But, oh, man, her expression nearly ripped his guts out. A beguiling mixture of innocence and seduction. Of temptation and redemption. He raised one of the bottles to his lips and took a long, slow drink.

He lowered the bottle and watched her trail behind her friend toward the bar. A line from one of those sappy romantic movies his mother loved to watch drifted through his mind. Of all the bars in the world, why did she have to walk into this one?

His heart thudded in his chest while he waited for her to reach him, but before she did, she touched her friend's elbow, said something he couldn't hear over the music, then steered her friend to the far end of the bar.

He couldn't believe she'd shown up in a dive like this. Even more surprising was the fact that no one else seemed to have noticed the princess of Palo Verde slumming in this joint. But maybe no one recognized her. After all, the bar's clientele seemed a far cry from the country club set she most likely usually hung out with.

He took another swig of beer, then worked his way back toward his brother, telling himself he was glad she'd avoided him. Just because she'd taken the leading role in every sexual fantasy he'd had in the past seven days didn't mean he wanted to run into her. Not with her dressed like that. And certainly not with his self-control so threadbare.

Plunking the bottle down in front of his brother, he scooted onto the opposite stool.

"Thanks, man." His brother took a swig of beer, then gestured with the bottle. "It's the damnedest thing. While you were up getting the beer, these two women walked in and I would've sworn one of them was that Sumners girl. You remember her from school?"

"No." He lied, because he didn't want to get into it.

"Man, she looks hot. Do you think she looked this hot back in school?"

"Nope." Hell, she hadn't looked this hot a week ago. And a week ago she'd been pressed up against his body, begging to be kissed, which had drastically increased her appeal.

Tomas took a fortifying drink, then set down the bottle and stood.

Alex reached out and grabbed his arm before he could get more than a step away. "Where're you going?"

Tomas pointed to the end of the bar where Jessica and her friend now lingered. Her friend, dressed in a skin-tight bright-red dress that crisscrossed her chest and left her belly bare, sat perched on the edge of a stool. Her elbows were propped on the bar behind her, a position that arched her back and thrust her breasts forward. Jessica stood off to the side, looking uncomfortable but still sexy as hell.

"I'm going over to say hello." Tomas grinned. "It'd be rude not to."

"Sit." He tried to keep the irritation from his voice, but didn't succeed.

"What?" Tomas asked. "You want a shot?"

At Jessica? Nope. He wasn't sure he could resist temptation again this soon.

"Look," he began hesitantly. "Jessica is—" Before he could fumble through an explanation, Tomas cut him off.

"Jessica, is it? You do remember her."

"She's thinking about having her kitchen remodeled. That's all."

Tomas raised his eyebrows. "That's all?"

Alex forced himself to nod, though he was tempted to do something considerably less benign. That was the kicker about family. They knew how to push your buttons. Tomas, the brother he was closest to both in age and temperament, certainly knew how to push his.

"If that's all it is, then you shouldn't mind if I go over to say hello." Tomas's smile broadened. "Should you?"

His desire to keep his brother away from Jessica battled with his instincts not to give in to Tomas's teasing. "Let it go, Tomas," he warned.

Tomas cocked his head in the direction of the bar. "Looks like I'll have to. Missed my chance."

Alex shifted in his chair to look over to where Jessica and her friend stood. While he and Tomas had been talking, the two women had drawn a small crowd.

A sinking feeling settled in his stomach. A guy so slick and glossy he looked like a magazine cover model wrapped his hands around the waist of Jessica's friend and lifted her to the bar. The woman smiled gamely, then swung her legs up onto the bar and stretched out. Propped up on her elbows, her chest thrust forward and her head tilted back, she commanded the attention of nearly every male in the room.

But not his. Alex's gaze went immediately to where he'd last seen Jessica. Thank God she was trying to move away from the bar instead of toward it. But the growing group of men crowded closer to where her friend lay sprawled and waiting…for tequila, no doubt.

Then, sure enough, the bartender approached with a bowl of limes and a bottle of the potent liquor. But Alex wasn't concerned about the girl on the bar. What worried him was the burly guy dressed in denim and flannel leering at Jessica.

A sinking feeling in Alex's gut told him that if he didn't step forward to stop it, the next woman lying across that bar would be Jessica.

4

"YOU'RE NEXT, sugar," a low voice growled in her ear.

Jessica jerked her gaze from the horrifying sight of Patricia balancing a shot of tequila on her belly for the next man in line.

The man wiped a dribble of liquor from his chin with the back of his hand. His still-moist lips twisted into a toothy smile.

Jessica pressed her fingers to her throat. "Me?"

"Yep, sweet thing, you're mine."

She stepped back, but bumped into the mass of men behind her. Scooting to her left, she tried to dissuade him. "Oh, I'm not sweet at all."

The redneck barked with laughter. "That's just fine. I like my women tart."

He reached for her and she darted to her right, barely eluding his grasping hands. "I'd really rather—"

A beefy hand grabbed her arm and yanked her toward him. "Now don't be shy."

Though her arms were trapped between them, she pressed her palms against his chest to leverage herself from his grasp. His shoulders were impossibly wide and he towered over her. Beneath her hands, his muscles felt like raw steaks, soft yet unyielding. Not raw steaks, she mentally corrected. Like an entire cow carcass. Huge, immovable and frankly rather nauseating.

She straightened her arms, straining to wiggle from his grasp. "I don't really like tequila," she protested.

He released another bark of laughter as his hands closed in on her waist. "You won't be drinking it," he said, as if that was reassuring.

He lifted her effortlessly and spun her toward the bar. She gasped as she landed on the hard—and somewhat sticky—wooden surface a few feet down from where Patricia still lay. Patricia's performance was drawing quite a crowd and almost no one noticed Jessica—or the redneck. Unfortunately the redneck's attention was riveted on her.

"Lonnie," the redneck called to the bartender, "another shot down here."

"Oh, my." She tried to scootch off the bar, but the redneck stood too close.

The bartender nodded to indicate he'd heard, but was busy pouring another drink. The delay bought her a few seconds to consider her fate. She patted the pocket of her Bolero jacket, where she'd stuffed two twenties, her keys and her pepper spray. She could talk her way out of this pickle, but she wanted it handy. Just in case.

But before she could even try the diplomatic approach, Alex elbowed his way toward her. He moved through the crush of people with the controlled grace of someone used to slipping through the unlit corners of the world.

For an instant, when his gaze met hers, she forgot where she was. The crowd, the redneck and even the impending tequila shot faded to little more than background noise as she watched him. For the first time since he'd come back, he seemed like the angry young man he'd been when he'd left. Wild and dangerous.

She jerked her gaze away and reality snapped back into place.

The bartender slapped a saltshaker, a bowl of limes and a shot glass down on the bar beside her hip. Tequila sloshed over the rim of the glass onto the bar and her bare thigh.

The redneck grabbed the bowl of limes and held it out to her. "Here ya go, honey."

The salacious gleam in his eyes churned her stomach. She pushed the bowl back toward him with her palm. "Thank you, but no."

Before the redneck could utter another word, Alex grabbed the bowl of limes from his hand.

"What the—"

"She's with me," Alex said, his voice hard and tight.

She tried to catch Alex's eye, but he didn't even glance her way.

The redneck bristled, his chest swelling with indignation. "She didn't come in with you."

Alex was lean, wiry. Even though he had to be nearly six feet tall—several inches taller than she was—the other guy dwarfed him, not just in height, but in width and mass, as well. Still, Alex didn't back down. Didn't even blink as he said, without glancing in her direction, "Jessica, tell him you're with me."

The redneck shot her a questioning look.

Talk about situations Emily Post never covered.

Any reply she might have made caught on her tongue and, ultimately, she could only nod mutely.

The rest of the bar carried on—loud and raucous, a turbulent whirl of people. Tension bounced between the three of them. They were like the quiet, deadly eye of the storm. Silent, tense and coiling for an explosion.

Her breath quickened and caught as she waited for one of the men to move. For one of them to back down. But neither did.

It was all she could do not to squeeze her eyes closed so she wouldn't have to watch. Alex was tough—she knew that—but this guy was huge. He was going to trample Alex. He would beat him to a pulp. He would—

Abruptly the guy shrugged, then shuffled a step back. He gave one last glance in her direction. "You sure you're with him?"

Before she could answer, Alex stepped forward. "Sure, she's sure." He placed his hand on her leg, just above her knee. "Aren't ya, honey?"

He didn't give her a chance to answer. Automatically her legs opened as he stepped between them. Bracing his hands on her hips, he pulled her toward him and gave her a hard, fast kiss. Just as she began arching into him, he pulled back, then ducked his head to nuzzle her neck.

Under the guise of nibbling her ear, he whispered, "What are you doing here?"

His lips felt divine against her skin and she shivered. Forcing herself not to arch into the caress, she struggled to focus on his words. And his exasperated tone.

"What are *you* doing here?" she countered.

"Saving your ass from Paul Bunyan, that's what."

Of course. He was rescuing her again. It wasn't that he'd changed his mind. It wasn't that he'd suddenly realized he found her irresistible. Annoyed with the way her pulse leaped at his touch, when clearly he wasn't affected at all, she snapped, "My ass doesn't need saving, thank you very much."

"You're in over your head," he insisted. She shoved at his shoulders. He didn't budge.

"I don't need to be rescued anymore. I was handling this just fine before you showed up." She'd hissed the words, so only he could hear.

He pulled back just far enough to look into her eyes. "You want to do body shots with Paul Bunyan, be my guest."

Paul Bunyan, it seemed, had been watching closely. He grabbed Alex's arm and pulled him around.

"I don't think she wants you here, after all."

Alex shrugged, his expression uninterested. "Well, Jess, what do you say? You want me to do the shot or you want him—" Alex tipped his head in Paul Bunyan's direction "—to do it?"

Her gaze darted from Alex's to Paul Bunyan's. Alex raised his eyebrow in question, Paul Bunyan looked torn between eyeing her hopefully and scowling at Alex.

What a choice!

No choice at all, really. She wasn't going to let Paul Bunyan put his moist, fat lips anywhere near her body, and Alex knew it. Damn him.

She watched him through narrowed eyes, wanting nothing more than to wipe that smug expression off his face.

Oh, you think you're so clever, don't you? Well, think again, mister.

He may have her backed into a corner, but that didn't mean she couldn't take him down with her.

Mimicking a move she'd watched Patricia pull earlier, she dropped her chin a notch so she gazed up at Alex from under her lashes. Twirling a single lock of hair around her finger, she said, "Alex, honey, of course I want you." He sucked in a breath of air and she blinked innocently up at him. "To do the shot, I mean."

She ran the toe of her boot up the outside of Alex's leg, smiling benignly up at Paul Bunyan. "You don't mind, do you? You'll still get to watch."

Paul Bunyan grinned broadly. "Just don't forget I'm here if you change your mind."

When she glanced back at Alex, she found him glowering at her. His grim expression almost made her laugh. That's what he got for trying to manipulate her.

Quickly on the heels of that thought came another.

She'd just manipulated him into doing a body shot off her in the middle of a crowded bar. Which was worse? The fact that he'd be kissing and licking her bare skin? Or the fact that he'd be doing it in public?

Well, she'd wanted to be bad. But how could she have known it would feel so good?

Glaring at her through narrowed eyes, he muttered, "Fine. Let's get this over with."

Pleased she'd gotten under his skin, she replied, perhaps a little too smugly, "Whenever you're ready."

Only when he quirked an eyebrow did she realize he was waiting for her to do something. For an instant her mind raced frantically. Patricia was the only person she'd ever seen do a body shot. She'd stretched out on the bar and had the salt poured on her bare belly. The stranger who'd done Patricia's shot had done a lot of licking. Something Jessica couldn't quite imagine letting any man do in public. Surely that wasn't the only way to go. After all, she'd seen those billboard ads for body shots…other body parts had been involved.

Determined to wing it, she slipped her jacket off her shoulders. She grabbed a lime from the bowl beside her and placed it on the hollow of her collarbone. She was less sure of what to do with the shot glass. So she merely held it in one hand and the saltshaker in the other.

She almost felt proud of herself. Until Alex stepped closer and licked the side of her neck. Instantly desire washed over her, sweeping away any other emotion she'd been feeling.

His tongue, moist and hot, swept down the side of her neck, lingering on the hollow at her collarbone. Then he grabbed the saltshaker from her hand and shook a generous sprinkling onto her neck. After the heat of his tongue, the salt felt surprisingly cool against her skin, which was so sensitized she seemed to feel each individual grain as it landed on her flesh. Heat pulsed through her body, settling low in her belly. Her skin prickled, ready for the touch of his tongue.

The crowd faded away as he pulled her closer, his hands firm and warm on her hips. Her eyes drifted closed as the heat of his breath washed across her skin. Time seemed to slow, the earth seemed to still, as she waited for him to lick the salt from her neck.

She'd expected a single swipe at the salt. Fast, like she'd seen that other man do on Patricia. Quick, like pulling off a Band-Aid. But, Alex, it seemed, was not a fast-and-quick man. He moved slowly, his tongue returning to her neck again and again in tiny passes, removing each grain of salt one at a time.

The room spun around her. She felt inexplicably unstable, as if she sat on a swing high above the crowd, rather than on the solid wooden bar. Her free hand automatically clutched at his shoulders as she sought to balance herself. But his assault on her senses continued and a single handhold couldn't keep her from slipping off the swing and plunging into the crowd. She clenched her knees together, pulling him closer, grounding herself in the moment.

His tongue lingered on her neck, prodding her pulse point over and over in a movement reminiscent of a much more intimate act. She shivered and gasped, arching toward him, nearly begging him to stop. Or to never stop, she wasn't quite sure which.

Then the licks turned to gentle soft kisses, no less potent. And then he stopped. For a moment he pressed his temple against her jaw. She could feel his thundering pulse beneath her chin, his ragged breath against her neck.

Abruptly he pulled away. His body tense and his movements sharp, he ducked his head to her collarbone and grabbed the slice of lime in his teeth. His lips brushed her shoulder as he bit down on the lime and a single drop of cool lime juice trickled onto her skin. He straightened, leaving the now-bruised lime still resting on her shoulder, and reached for the shot glass.

He tossed back the shot with a single drink, then slammed the glass down beside her on the bar. The clang of the glass against wood—which sounded remarkably loud in the already loud room—snapped her senses back into place.

As if waking abruptly from a dream, she was instantly aware of everything around her. The hum of dance music, the scents of stale perfume and staler beer, the mass of people around them—some watching their display, most unaware of their existence. And of Alex…standing so close, his expression taut and his normally dark eyes nearly black.

Worst of all, she was aware of her own position, perched on the bar, her legs nearly wrapped around a man who was—for all intents and purposes—a stranger.

Oh, my.

Oh, my goodness.

This may not have been on The List, but it should have been, because she definitely felt *Saucy* now.

She wanted to pull Alex back into her arms and lick off whatever tequila still clung to his lips. To hell with propriety. To hell with society's expectations for Jessica Sumners.

Before that kernel of rebellion could muster enough force to even mount a protest, Alex's eyes narrowed.

He didn't step away from her. Didn't so much as move an inch, but she felt his withdrawal just the same.

Grabbing her hips, he lifted her from the bar as if she weighed no more than the shot glass. He set her on the ground, then grabbed her hand. "Come on, let's get out of here."

But she sensed from his clenched jaw and brusque attitude that this was not the start of the hot fling she'd been hoping for. She might have tempted him, but now he was back to rescuing her. More's the pity.

Still, she had more sense than to protest, and let him pull her blindly along toward the door. He stopped just short of the door to talk to a man seated at one of the tables. She assumed he was one the brothers Alex'd mentioned, since he had the same high cheekbones and piercing eyes as Alex. Desperate to regain some of her usual control, she moved around Alex and extended her hand. "I'm Jessica. I don't believe we've met."

Tomas stood, smiling, and took her hand. "Tomas. Alex's brother."

"I figured." She smiled in return, secretly thrilled he didn't bother to hide his appreciation.

Alex, however, seemed less than pleased. "You can let go of her hand now."

Tomas's smile broadened as he released her hand. "A bit of a bully, isn't he?"

She smiled. "Most definitely."

To Alex he said, "You go on. I'll be fine here."

Alex nodded, "Thanks."

He pulled her just a few steps toward the door before she protested. "I came with Patricia. I drove her here. I can't just leave without her."

"I suspect Patricia will be just fine on her own."

"But I can't leave her," she stated again. There were probably all kinds of protocols that she didn't know about going clubbing with single friends. But even if that protocol said it was okay to leave your friends stranded at a club, she just couldn't do it.

"Fine." The word came out as little more than a growl. "Go find her."

For a moment Jessica stared at him, eyes wide. Alex felt the energy that had been buzzing back and forth between them all night—hell, since he'd walked into her house last week—intensify like the thrumming feedback of an amplifier turned up too loud. Then she spun on her heel and disappeared into the crowd.

Just let her go, his mind begged. *Just let her walk the hell away.*

He didn't even bother to argue with himself over it. No way would he leave her here alone. Not with this crowd, already rough, on edge and more than a little drunk. Not when he knew what every guy here was thinking. He knew what they were thinking, because he was thinking the same damn thing. In vivid Technicolor detail.

But there were two major differences between him and every other guy in here. One, his fantasies were fueled by the memory of what it was like to actually taste that beautiful skin. And two, he was the only man in the room determined to keep his distance.

5

THOUGH THE CROWD was thick, he easily kept her in his sights. Her blond hair was too distinctive to miss. She wasn't the only blonde in the club, but she was the only one on whom the honey tones looked natural. He caught up with her just in time to send a warning scowl at one of the fools lumbering toward her.

She stopped just short of the dance floor. Standing on her tippy toes, she strained to see over the crowd. Pointing to the far corner of the room, he said, "Over there."

He knew the instant she spotted her friend in the throes of a complicated bump and grind between two guys, because she recoiled and stumbled into him. She'd tried so hard to be tough and worldly tonight. And she was failing so miserably.

An unexpected wave of protectiveness washed over him. She didn't belong here any more than he belonged in her world. And he could only imagine how he would feel at one of her society parties. He battled the sudden urge to carry her away from all this. To protect her.

But from what? From his world? From himself?

Before he could do—or say—anything stupid, she straightened her shoulders and marched onto the dance floor. He could do nothing other than follow. She approached the dancers with a confused but determined expression on her face.

Finally she brushed past one of Patricia's male admirers to tap Patricia on the shoulder. Patricia smiled broadly as she greeted Jessica.

From this noisy corner of the dance floor, he couldn't hear what the two women said, but their body language spoke clearly enough. Jessica suggesting they leave. Patricia brushing aside Jessica's offer for a ride. Repeat as needed.

Finally, Jessica turned back to him. Bracing her hand on his upper arm, she stood on her toes to speak into his ear. "She doesn't want to go."

"Obviously." He grabbed her hand, ostensibly to lead her toward the door, but also to keep her from touching him. There was only so much a guy could take.

But she stood firm. "I can't just leave her here."

Ah, crap. Here we go again.

He was just about to launch an argument when he spotted Paul Bunyan watching them from his perch near the bar. Great. Just what they needed.

Alex tightened his hold on Jessica's fingers and pulled her closer. "Dance with me."

"What?"

Before she could pull away, he wrapped his other arm around her waist and pressed her to his chest. Thrown off balance, she leaned against him. His hands settled low on her hips, instinctively pulling her closer.

His body leaped to life at her nearness and the erection he'd just started to get under control strained against his jeans. His mind flashed back to how her lips had felt under his. For a moment all he could think of was how damn good it would feel to let his hands slip down to the hem of her skirt. To ease that hem up and expose the silky skin of her thighs to his touch. To make love to her right here.

To lose himself so completely in her that he forgot they were in a public place.

Trying to distract himself, he started dancing, slowly shifting his feet. However, Jessica's feet remained firmly rooted to the ground.

She stared up at him, her wide eyes filled with confusion. "What are you doing?"

What was he doing? "Dancing. You can't stand in the middle of the dance floor arguing. People notice." He nodded in the direction of Paul Bunyan. "I didn't want our friend over there to get any more ideas."

She glanced back over to the bar. "Oh."

"You know, this dancing thing will look more convincing if you dance with me."

Slowly her feet shifted back and forth between his. The action created just enough friction between their bodies to drive him crazy. He forced himself to continue the conversation they'd been having before he'd spotted Paul Bunyan. "If Patricia doesn't want to come with you, you don't have a choice." He sounded far more reasonable than he felt.

"The thing is, she has it in her head that she doesn't want to leave alone, you know? She made me promise that we wouldn't leave until we'd both picked up guys. I tried to tell her that you hadn't really picked me up—that you were just taking me home—but she didn't believe me."

Well, at least he knew where he stood with her now. To her, going home with him didn't count as being picked up. "So leave her here." He practically ground the words out.

She pressed her palms against his chest to push away from him. "I still can't leave her here."

"Jessica—" He growled the warning.

"Look, you don't want to stay? Fine. Don't stay. But

I'm not leaving without Patricia. So if you'll kindly let go of me…"

Even though she was a good three inches shorter than he was, she managed to look down her nose at him. How the hell she could stand there, dressed like that, and still look like the princess of some snotty European principality he'd never know.

The only thing he did know was that he sure as hell wasn't going to leave her royal highness alone in this bar. "Fine. I'll get Tomas to take her home," he muttered, dragging her away from the dance floor toward Tomas's table.

"But—"

"Don't worry. He'll get her home safely and without bruising her ego."

A few minutes later he shoved Jessica into the empty chair beside a smirking Tomas. "Wait here. I'll go get Patricia." To Tomas, he said, "Don't let her out of your sight."

Tomas's smile broadened.

Alex scowled and resisted the temptation to knock his brother off the chair. He wasn't feeling any friendlier when he finally extracted Patricia from her admirers and dragged her back to the table twenty minutes later.

Tomas and Jessica sat side by side, their heads bent toward each other as they talked. From across the room, he saw Jessica tilt her head, turn her ear closer to Tomas, concentration written clearly on her face. Her eyes widened in surprised amusement as she got the punch line to whatever joke or story Tomas was telling her. Then she laughed.

A full-bellied, throw-your-head-back laugh.

Watching them together, something ugly and unpleasant twisted in his stomach. Something very unbrotherly.

Something he definitely shouldn't be feeling in connection with a woman who meant nothing to him.

His relationship with Tomas had all the standard childhood crap that came with a large family. But even at its absolute worst, he'd never felt like this. This gut-wrenching jealousy. All because Tomas had made Jessica laugh.

Only when he felt Patricia pulling on his arm did he realize he'd stopped walking. The sight of Jessica and his brother had literally stopped him cold.

"Aren't we going?" Patricia trilled loudly.

Angry with himself for being jealous in the first place and for being so damn transparent, he snapped, "Sure."

He deposited Patricia unceremoniously into Tomas's care and dragged Jessica out the door without waiting to see if they would follow. Stopping short outside the door, he scanned the parking lot for the cherry-red Beemer he'd seen parked in her driveway the other day. He found it, parked all alone in the far corner, as if the car had been afraid of catching cooties from the other cars.

He stomped off in the direction of her car, assuming Jessica would follow and almost too irritated to care if she didn't. What the hell was wrong with him?

He was still asking himself that same question as Jessica began insisting on driving, but he ignored her.

"Fine!" she finally said, throwing open the passenger door and climbing inside.

Once behind the wheel, he felt a moment's hesitation. Why couldn't she have driven a Toyota or Volvo? No, the princess had to drive a top-of-the-line convertible M3. The damn thing was worth more than his house.

Scanning the interior of the car, he struggled to orient himself with the different controls of a foreign vehicle. He'd borrowed a friend's Yugo once in L.A., but that was as close as he'd gotten to a German-engineered automobile. The fine-grain leather seat cradled his body and, once he'd eased the seat back a couple of notches to accommodate his longer legs, he realized this was going to be—hands down—the most comfortable, most exhilarating drive he'd ever take.

He glanced at the gearshift, straining to see it in the dimly lit interior. Six Speeds. Damn. Forget comfortable. This was gonna be a blast.

"I told you I should drive," she muttered as if reading his mind.

"I can handle it," he muttered as he slipped the car into Reverse and backed out of the spot. The bar was on the far outskirts of town and they were a good twenty or thirty minutes from either of their homes.

After a moment of silence she said, "So, you never told me how you got into construction."

"You never asked," he pointed out. A little of his irritation began to slide away. Jessica clearly found the situation awkward and it amused him that she was trying to make polite conversation.

Her lips curved downward. Frowning, but more irritated than annoyed. "Are you always this difficult?"

"Are you always this nosy?"

"Only when I'm uncomfortable," she blurted.

He took his eyes off the road long enough to glance in her direction. In the flickering light of the street lamps, he noticed her stiff posture, her tightly clenched hands. She met his gaze and he cocked an eyebrow in question.

"Conversational sleight of hand," she said with a nervous laugh.

"Excuse me?"

"You ask people questions, get them talking about

themselves." At his pointed look she added, "My parents had political aspirations since before I was born. I grew up needing to know how to make conversation." She shifted to look out the window, so he almost didn't hear her sigh. "The easiest way to keep people entertained is to keep them talking about themselves."

He pondered that for a minute, wondering what it must have been like to grow up under those circumstances. Wondered if that was why she'd been so serious as a teenager. Their lives had been so different. And for the first time he considered that hers—for all its wealth and acceptability—might not have been easy.

"That must have been a hard way to grow up," he found himself saying.

"I suppose it was." Then after a minute she added, "I think it was easier on my brother. He made a great politician's son. You know, class president, football hero, that kind of thing. But I would have been happier just sitting on the sidelines and staying out of the limelight. Thus the need for the conversational sleight of hand."

Her words were so different from what he would have expected of her. And yet, was it really that surprising? The girl who had left notes in his locker all those years ago had seemed unsure and a little shy. She had talked, even then, about wanting to escape from the shadow of her father's presence. She had spoken of parents who loved her but whose reputation and expectations were stifling. He'd known all too well what that was like.

Because he didn't know what else to say, he answered the question she'd asked earlier. "My uncle worked in construction. Carpentry, actually. He lives in Sacramento, but he did work here in Palo Verde, also. Remember when the country club was remodeled back in the eighties? He did a lot of the woodwork on that."

"So after graduation you went to work for him?"

"I started working with him when I was twelve. Over the weekends, during the summer."

"That isn't legal!" She sounded outraged.

"Probably not." He shrugged as he slipped the car into a higher gear. "At a busy construction site, people don't notice a boy doing odd jobs, hauling away scraps and carrying lumber."

"And your parents let you do this?"

"My father insisted." She understood so little of what his life had been like, so he tried to explain. "Migrant farm workers don't make a lot of money. A lot of kids go to work at ten or eleven to help out. But my parents wouldn't let any of us drop out of school. Even when they finally let me start working, they wanted me to have a skill."

"I…" Her voice cracked under the weight of her obvious remorse. "I didn't know. I'm sorry."

"Don't apologize."

"But I didn't mean to imply—"

"Look, I'm not ashamed of my parents. I'm proud of all they did. They worked hard. And they kept us together. They made sure we got an education. They wanted us to have the sort of success they'd never had. I don't want to do anything to jeopardize that."

"When I said I was sorry, I wasn't apologizing for your background, I was apologizing for my ignorance."

He nodded. Again she'd surprised him. He didn't like how off balance he felt around her.

As if trying to put distance between himself and his desire, he slipped her car into sixth gear, enjoying the thrum of the engine responding to his command.

"You like it, don't you?"

He shot her a suspicious look. "Like what?"

"Driving the Beemer." In the light of a passing street-lamp, he saw her smile…the first genuine smile she'd given him all night. "You're enjoying the power, aren't you?"

He did enjoy it. Handling this high-performance car gave him a bigger thrill than he ever would have imagined. Part of him wanted to remember every second of this drive, knowing he'd never again get the chance to put his hands on a car quite like this one.

And part of him knew he'd trade the experience in an instant for the chance to get his hands on Jessica again.

She intrigued him unlike any woman he'd ever known. She seemed a mass of contradictions. One minute so serious, the next so sexy. He wanted to peel back the layers of her personality to reveal the true Jessica, almost as much as he wanted to peel back the layers of her clothes. What few layers she still wore.

Pulling his thoughts back to the car he said, "Actually, I'm surprised you enjoy driving the Beemer. You don't strike me as a standard kind of girl."

She laughed. Unlike the laughter she'd shared with his brother, this laugh didn't sound amused, but tinged with relief.

"Funny, that's what my mom said." She raised her voice and spoke in a snooty tone. "Do you really have to drive that—that sports car? How would it look for your father if you were stopped and given a speeding ticket?"

He shifted the car into a lower gear. If her mother thought it would look bad getting caught speeding, he could just imagine how she'd feel about Jessica's car being pulled over with Alex Moreno driving.

"So you never speed," he observed.

Her smile broadened and mischief glinted in her eyes. "I just never get caught."

"Good planning."

"It's all about knowing where the cops are." Her voice sounded dreamy, as if she ached to be behind the wheel now, zipping along at eighty miles an hour. "The cops spend the whole weekend patrolling the highway between Sacramento and Lake Tahoe. Which leaves the northern part of the county free. There are some great back roads up in the foothills. If you get out there early enough on Saturday or Sunday morning, there's not a soul around."

"Rock Creek Road."

Her head snapped toward him. "You know it?"

"I used to go driving there when I was a kid." He stopped at a light and turned to look at Jessica. In the moonlight her hair seemed even paler. The light changed and he forced his attention back to the road.

"When you were a kid?" she asked.

"Well, teenager."

"In your '69 Camaro."

"That's right." It'd been a rusted-out piece of junk when he'd bought it, in such bad shape even he'd been able to afford it.

"Man, I loved that car." The day he'd scraped together the money to buy it had been one of the proudest of his young life.

"I know," she murmured. "The speed. The power. It's like flying."

Her words were filled with pure, unadulterated joy. He could picture her, in his mind, speeding along the hairpin turns of Rock Creek Road, the top down on her car, the wind blowing through that glorious blond hair of hers. The bright noonday sun shining down on her.

His own experiences on Rock Creek Road had been very different. And not just because he'd been driving a beat-up old Camaro instead of a high-performance, sixty-thousand-dollar luxury car.

He'd always gone at night—the darker the better. For him, there'd been no joy in driving along Rock Creek Road. Only escape. Disappearing in the darkness. Driving had been an act of rebellion. And of freedom, yes. But not of joy.

He struggled to put that into words and, in the end, gave up. His emotions seemed so...ugly compared to hers. "For me it was the solitude."

"The solitude?"

"Six kids in a three-bedroom house."

"Oh." She looked horrified, but tried to hide it. "I hadn't thought... That's a lot of people under one roof. I guess you needed the escape, too."

Escape, too, she'd said, which left him wondering what exactly *she* was escaping from. That wonderful life of hers? That life of wealth and privilege that he'd always assumed was so perfect, but apparently wasn't?

Even though he knew it was a mistake to bring it up, he still found himself saying, "So, going to the club tonight...was that another thing from your list?"

"Yeah, I guess so."

"But...?" he prodded.

She twisted to look out the window. "There is no but."

"You're working your way through that list like there's no tomorrow. This can't just be about some magazine article."

"No, the magazine article just made me realize how tired I was of settling for less than what I want."

"Tell me something, Jess. Do you like your job? Are you good at it?"

"I'll be a great manager. If I ever get the promotion."

"No. The job you do now. Do you like that one?"

"Programming?" She sounded surprised by his question. "Yes, I do. I'm good at it. Writing code and debugging it appeals to me."

"If you like what you do now, why are you so determined to get that promotion?"

"I—" She broke off, and he could sense her confusion.

After a long, thoughtful moment, she answered him. "Just expectations, I guess. I'm nearing thirty and I don't feel like I've accomplished much."

He raised his eyebrows. "You went to college. You have your own house. You're good at a job you like doing. What more do you want?"

"It's not that simple. Not for a Sumners anyway. My father was a judge by the time he was thirty. He went on to parlay that into a career in politics and now he's a senator. My brother owns his own consulting business. He was worth over a million dollars by the time he was thirty. It's a lot of live up to."

"And you think your parents love him more because of all he's achieved?"

"No," she said quickly, but then added, "Not exactly. They've always been proud of his accomplishments. But with me it was different. I was always their little girl. They were always trying to protect me. As if I couldn't handle things on my own."

"And you always hated that," he murmured, without meaning to say it out loud, and he felt her stiffen beside him.

"Yes, I did. How did you know that?"

"From the, um—" he cleared his throat "—the notes you wrote. There was one about some concert in Sacramento they wouldn't let you and some friends go to. You were pretty pissed at them."

"I can't believe you remember that."

Even without so much as glancing in her direction, he felt the intensity of her stare. Uncomfortable under her scrutiny, he shrugged it off. "It just came back to me now."

But in truth, he remembered every note she'd sent him—seventeen in all—almost to the word. He'd reread them dozens, maybe hundreds, of times. Late at night, after the rest of his family had gone to bed, he'd sneak out to his car, turn on the dome light and reread her notes. As he'd sat there in that grungy, beat-up, piece-of-junk Camaro he'd loved so much, he'd imagine her writing those notes to him. He imagined her sitting in the middle of her bed—one of those fancy, ruffly, four-poster jobs— propped up on mounds of pillows, her soft blond hair loose around her shoulders, looking like some princess from one of the fairy tales his mother made him read in English to his younger sisters.

"I remember the things you wrote me, too." Her words spilled out quickly. As though she was embarrassed by the admission. "You never complained about your family."

"Not much to complain about." At least, not much that she'd have understood. Or that he could have told her without revealing how dirt poor they really were. He couldn't tell her how tired he'd gotten of eating rice and beans. Or how he'd dreaded the end of apple season when his family would pick up and move to Arizona for a couple of months each winter. So instead, he'd crafted his notes from his hopes and dreams.

"You always talked about the places you wanted to

travel," she said. "The things you wanted to do when you got out of school. I think that's why I loved your notes. Your future was wide open. No expectations. No settling."

But that had been big talk back then. What he wanted now was so much simpler than that. Just a decent job that made decent money and that people respected him for doing.

Wanting to shift the focus back to her, he asked, "But what about what you want? You said you don't want to settle. So don't."

She drifted into silence and he wondered if he'd offended her. Then suddenly she chuckled. "Thank you."

"For what?"

"For trying to make me feel better. And for getting me out of there."

Glancing into his rearview mirror to make sure there were no other cars on the road, he slowed down and pulled off the main highway onto a darkened side road. As the car came to halt, he shifted into neutral and set the hand brake.

He turned in his seat to face her. "Jess, you shouldn't ever have to settle."

Jessica twisted in her seat, tucking one foot behind the calf of her other leg. The movement was intrinsically classy. A reminder she was a princess, despite her clothes. And way out of his league.

But that didn't stop him from wanting her. An odd intimacy settled over them, brought on by the close confines of the car and dim dashboard lighting. His headlights stretched out into the night outside, but inside, the world seemed to contract to include just the two of them.

"I…" She bit down on her lip and he thought there was a glimmer of tears in her eyes. "Thank you."

Her intense vulnerability damn near broke his heart.

He exhaled a deep, slow breath, then brushed his thumb against her chin, working up to her lip. With a gentle tug, he pulled her lip free from her teeth. "Ah, Jess, you're killing me."

He hadn't meant it as an invitation, but nor did he stop her when she leaned forward and pressed her lips to his. Her kiss was tentative and shy. And unbelievably erotic.

She tasted sweet and hot with just a hint of mint. Like she'd brushed her teeth before leaving the house and the flavor still lingered. Proof she hadn't even had a drink at the bar. This close, she smelled faintly of limes, a scent he'd never considered erotic until now. But the scent called up the memory of how her skin had felt beneath his tongue. Smooth and silky. Far more potent than the shot of tequila.

6

HE'D HAD ENOUGH trouble keeping his hands off her when he'd made himself think of her as a rich, selfish princess. Now that he knew the truth, he didn't stand a chance.

He knew in an instant if he didn't pull away now, he'd be in serious trouble. No matter how much he wanted her, he couldn't have her. She was all wrong for him. And there was no way he could get involved with her without destroying any chance he had of making this town believe he wasn't the reckless and wild boy he'd been when he'd left ten years ago. Worse still, the decent man Jessica thought he was would walk away from her right now.

That thought alone gave him the strength to pull away from the temptation of her kiss.

He gripped her upper arms, gently setting her aside. "We can't do this."

She looked up at him, her eyes wide, pupils dilated in the dim lighting. "Why not?"

"Look, Jessica, don't think I'm not interested, but I really can't." He held her gaze, hoping she'd see the truth in his eyes. "I'm trying to run a business. I've got enough going against me as it is."

She frowned, looking adorably confused. "I don't understand."

No, she probably didn't. She was blind to the inequality in Palo Verde. Not because she purposely ignored it the way so many people did, but because she just didn't think that way.

"How do you think people would feel about me if we were together?" he asked her.

"I don't know." She cocked her head to the side considering. "I don't think I care. Surely you don't, either. That kind of thing has never mattered to you."

"Fifteen years ago, you'd have been right. But things are different now. I've got a business."

"You think being seen with me would hurt your business?"

He laughed, a chuckle half amusement, half resignation. "Soil the reputation of Senator Sumners's precious daughter? Hell, yes, I think that would hurt my business."

"But why? I don't understand."

"People like you, Jessica. They feel protective toward you. It's like you're the freakin' town mascot or something."

She scowled, looking seriously displeased with the analogy. "Maybe you're wrong. Maybe being with me would help. I know a lot of people in this town. Besides, people here have better things to worry about than my social life."

"Maybe. But there's a good chance it would just piss people off. I don't want to make it harder than it has to be."

"No offense, but if it's so hard, why are you doing it? Why start a business here? Why move back here at all?"

Wasn't that the million-dollar question? Alex exhaled slowly. "Making it here, it's just something I have to do. Something I have to prove to myself. When I left town after high school, it wasn't by choice."

She nodded, her expression serious but without censure. "I always wondered if the rumors were true."

"Rumors?"

"That after high school you'd been arrested. For fighting. And that you had pulled a knife on the guy."

"Actually, I just had a pocketknife. The police found it when they patted me down. Who knows if that would have factored into the charges."

"But instead of filing charges, they just brought you before the judge…"

Her voice trailed off. Either she didn't know what had happened after that, or she didn't want to say, so he finished the story for her. "He suggested I leave town."

"'Suggested'? That doesn't sound like Daddy."

"Daddy?"

She blushed and averted her eyes. "The judge. It was him, wasn't it? This was before he ran for Senate when he handled cases like this."

"It was him. And you're right. 'Suggested' probably isn't the right word. He said I'd be better off starting over some other place."

She frowned. "I'm not sure I understand. 'Some other place'?"

"Some place where I had less of a history."

More importantly, some place where he'd had less of a history with the judge's daughter. It had gone unsaid back then, and so he left it unsaid now. There was no reason to make Jessica feel bad over something that had happened years ago. Something she'd had no control over in the first place.

She puzzled over his words for a minute, then said, "So my father wanted you to leave town so you could get a clean start somewhere else?" She studied him, then added, "But you don't think that's the real reason he did it, do you?"

He wanted to prevaricate, but found it difficult to do so with her watching. "Let's just say I think he may have taken other issues into consideration and leave it at that."

"'Other issues'? What other issues?"

Other issues such as Alex's relationship with Jessica. "Let's leave it at that," he repeated.

Not that he and Jessica had had a relationship back then. It was all speculation and gossip. Speculation and gossip that might have become public record if Alex had ever gone to trial. Could he really blame the judge for using his power to make sure that hadn't happened?

The judge had made it clear he thought substantiating the rumors about their relationship would ruin Jessica's life. Maybe he'd been right.

Jessica studied him, as if trying to decide how far she could push it or whether or not she should leave it at that. Thankfully, she let it drop. Sort of.

"My father, for all his faults, is a fair man. Dictatorial, yes, but fair. He may have genuinely thought he was acting in your best interests." She must have seen the doubt in his eyes, because she rushed on before he could interrupt. "And taking care of the people of this town has always been his top priority."

"My parents are migrant farm workers. Don't assume your father thought of me as one of this town's citizens."

"I don't believe that. My father—"

"Your father saw me the same way everyone else in town did. As a wild, reckless pain in the ass that would probably end up in jail someday anyway."

She studied him, her gaze serious and relentlessly probing. "Is that why you moved back here? To prove they were all wrong? To prove to everyone that you made something of yourself and you didn't end up in jail?"

"Yeah, I guess so."

Suddenly she looked up, her expression brighter. "But you said you're having trouble finding work."

"All I need is one really good job," he said with more bravado than he felt. "Construction is like any other business. It's all about networking. One job leads to the next."

"What about the courthouse?" she asked, her tone bright.

"The county courthouse?"

"Yes. In the last election, the county passed a bond to renovate the building. I know all about it because Daddy had me working overtime at the country club to campaign for support. It's a huge job. If you got it, you'd be set."

He'd been running some numbers in his spare time, but knew getting the job was a long shot. And that was if he could convince the powers that be he was a reformed man.

And then there was Jessica, staring up at him with her bright blue eyes. Whether she knew it or not, every flicker of her gaze, every flutter of her well-manicured fingertips transmitted a sensual promise. He'd like nothing more than to peel off her clothes and explore every inch of her sleek little body.

But those were not the actions of a reformed man.

Besides, she wanted a plaything. A check on her list. Nothing more. He told himself he wanted her just because she was available. Just because nailing her would bring that teenage fantasy of his to life. Yet, deep down inside, he was afraid it was more than that. And if there was one thing he knew about rich girls, when they tired of their playthings, they tossed them aside.

Since she still seemed to be waiting for an answer, he said, "I'm already looking into it."

She watched him carefully, as if gauging his reaction. "You don't think you'll get, do you?"

Because she was right, he didn't answer directly. Instead he asked, "Why do you say that?"

"All those things you said about how hard it's been for you to start a business in this town... You were talking about bidding the job for the courthouse, weren't you? That's what you meant."

Seeing the determined glint in her gaze, he admitted what she already knew. "It's harder than I thought it would be. I didn't realize how many people here still think I'm worthless."

"Not worthless," she protested. "Just wild."

"Too wild to finish a job."

"I could help you. Put in a good word with my father. *He* could help you."

"Helping me is the last thing your father will want to do. Trust me on that."

"Look, he has his faults, believe me, I know. And I may not always agree with the way he and my mom do things, but if I ask him to, I'm sure he'll help. He can convince people you've changed..." Her voice trailed off, as if she'd become lost in thought. After a moment she said, "But it wouldn't help if people thought we were sleeping together, would it?"

He shook his head. "Nope."

"I see." Twisting in her seat, she shifted her leg back to the floor and turned as if to look out the window.

Watching her in profile, he could see her struggle to breathe and knew she was as affected by this intimacy as he was. He, too, twisted back in his seat. He shifted the car into first and executed a perfect three-point turn before he realized how tightly he was gripping the steering wheel.

Forcing his hands to loosen, he said, "After tonight, we probably shouldn't see each other again."

From the corner of his gaze, he saw her nod stiffly. "Of course."

As he pulled back onto the highway, the frustration eating away at him mingled with anger. Anger at himself.

Kissing Jessica had been a mistake. A big one.

Kissing her only made him yearn for all the things he couldn't have. And right now, she topped that list.

But he'd said it himself. She should never have to settle. And if the two of them ever did get involved, they'd both be settling. She'd have to settle for a man who wasn't good enough for her and he'd have to settle for being just the man she slept with. He didn't want either of them to make that sacrifice.

7

CUTIE PIES held the dubious honor of being Palo Verde's most popular restaurant. Located on Main Street, half a mile west of the county courthouse, between Hansen's Hardware, est. 1894, and Cash Down Bail Bonds, est. 1987. Every morning the local apple farmers came in to eat breakfast and to complain about the codling moths. By lunchtime, the place was full of judges and attorneys. Directly across the street sat the Palo Verde Hotel, the oldest continually operating hotel in the Northern Valley where, occasionally, celebrities stayed on their way through town to Lake Tahoe.

So while Cutie Pies made its money selling pastries, coffee and light lunches, its real trade was in gossip. Something every girl born and bred in Palo Verde knew quite well. But Jessica had spent her entire life being immune to the local gossip mill—not because her character was so sterling, but because she, quite frankly, had never done anything interesting enough to warrant gossip.

What Alex had said about the way the town viewed her had got her thinking. What if everyone did just see her as Judge Sumners's precious daughter? What if that was part of the problem? Maybe she'd been such a good girl all her life simply because everyone always treated her like a good girl.

That had certainly been true back in high school when boyfriends had always brought her home from dates at nine fifty-five and no one ever invited her to keg parties. But was it still true?

She'd never done anything to change the way people viewed her. Until now.

So when she walked into Cutie Pies just after ten o'clock on Saturday morning, she missed the way the restaurant went silent. She also ignored the inquiring look from Mrs. Frankfort, the sixty-year-old woman who ran Cutie Pies and taught the local tai chi class. Nor did she notice the pointed way the waitress asked her how her morning was when she ordered her latte and her low-fat oatmeal muffin. In fact she didn't notice anything until she turned to leave, her muffin tucked safely in a white paper bag, and saw Alex sitting at a far table with his brother Tomas, the remnants of bacon, eggs and a short stack sitting in front of them while they finished their coffee.

Her heart leaped at the sight of him, but her feet simply stopped moving. For a moment she just stood there, clutching her coffee and her little white bag.

She'd spent a lot of time the previous night thinking about their conversation in the car. Oh, he was attracted to her, all right. After that tequila shot, there was no way he could deny it. He wanted her.

Ultimately she was right back where she'd been before she'd gone to the bar. With one exception. Now she knew what she wanted. Alex. And she wasn't going to take no for an answer.

She had briefly considered his concerns about the town thinking he'd "corrupted her," but then dismissed them. He was wrong about that. She knew the people of this town much better than he did. Being with her would do far more to help his career than to hurt it.

She wanted—no, needed—to see where this thing with Alex would lead. She needed to know if she could ever be the kind of woman he couldn't walk away from.

He'd said she wasn't his type, but that could change. She'd just have to discover what his type was.

Determined to do just that, she crossed the diner to Alex's table. His expression tightened and he didn't look particularly pleased to see her. Tomas, however, immediately stood and asked her to join them.

As she lowered herself to one of the vacant chairs, Alex's frown deepened. "I don't think this is a good idea."

"It's just breakfast," Tomas said.

But Jessica knew what Alex meant. It wasn't a good idea because people might gossip about them, gossip that might hurt his chances of getting work. But Jessica had a plan to change all that.

Before she could reassure Alex, Tomas said, "I think I'll head back over to the house. You can stay here and finish your breakfast."

Before Alex could protest, she smiled brightly and said, "Thanks. That'd be great."

Alex scowled at her but waited until Tomas was out the door before leaning forward, propping his elbow on the table and saying in a low voice, "Jess, this isn't a good time."

"Don't worry. I have a plan."

He gazed at her from under half-lowered lids, clearly suspicious. "What plan?" he asked.

"I want you to remodel my kitchen." Feeling smug, she pulled her muffin from the bag, then refolded the paper flat and set the muffin on top.

"Why? A week ago you couldn't have cared less."

"A girl can't change her mind?"

"Let's just say I suspect your motives."

"Fine." She carefully peeled back the paper baking cup and broke off a piece of the crunchy top. "That's fair. But you need the money. And I need change."

"Pity? You're doing this out of pity?"

"I hadn't thought of it like that." She tilted her head to the side and considered that as she nibbled on her muffin. Then she firmly shook her head. "Well, it's not out of pity. Guilt? Maybe. But not pity."

"Guilt?"

"I feel bad for the way I treated you. Especially since you've been so nice to me."

He shifted uncomfortably in his chair, reaching for his coffee cup only to realize it was empty. He set it down with a loud thump and an irritated, "Humph."

A pretty young waitress zipped to his side with the coffeepot. "You want a refill, sugar?"

"Sure." But he didn't even look in the waitress's direction.

Jessica popped a bite of muffin into her mouth to hide her smile. Even when he was looking annoyed, it felt darn good to be the center of Alex's attention.

As soon as the woman left, he said, "I won't take your money. I don't care how guilty you feel."

"Ah, but you're the one who said I shouldn't settle."

Alex looked confused. "Huh?"

"Last night, you said I should never settle. Well, I've never liked the kitchen as it is now. It's boring and drab. So I want a new kitchen and I'm not going to settle for anything less than the best." She met his gaze with wide-eyed innocence. "You are the best, aren't you, Alex?"

He merely glowered at her, as if he knew exactly where this was going.

"Besides," she continued in a cheerful voice. "It's on The List."

"You expect me to believe that 'have your kitchen remodeled' is on *Saucy* magazine's list of '10 Things Every Woman Should Do'?"

She laughed, swatting at his arm. "No, silly. But number nine on The List is 'Shake Up Your Space.' I figure a kitchen remodel counts."

He sipped his coffee—black, she noticed—while studying her over the rim of the white ceramic mug. Finally he shook his head. "Can't let you do it."

"But—"

"If you spend all this money just because of some stupid list, you'll regret it in the end."

"I won't," she insisted. Planting her palms on the table, she leaned forward. "I need to do this."

"Why?"

"Because it's time. I haven't done a single reckless and irresponsible thing in my entire life."

He chuckled. "There's a sixty-thousand-dollar car parked out on the street that says differently."

"I bought it used and got a very good deal." Then she realized how ridiculous that sounded. "Okay, so maybe buying a used convertible and having my kitchen remodeled aren't the wildest things I could do, but it's a step in the right direction."

His lips curved in a sardonic smile, all trace of annoyance now gone.

"A very small step," she admitted. "Besides, if you're not working for me, no one will believe me when I recommend you for jobs."

"You're going to recommend me?"

"Naturally. You said it yourself. One job will lead to the

next. And I know a lot of people in this town. The right people."

"'The right people'?"

A flicker of disgust crossed his face and she wished she'd picked a different word. "The people who can help you get this job remodeling the courthouse. Look, the courthouse is classified as a historic building. That means everything about the remodel has to be approved by the historical society. The architect, the plans, the builder. Everything."

"Please tell me you're kidding."

"That's the bad news. The good news is, if you can win over the historical society, you're in."

"Trust me," he muttered, "that's not the good news."

"That's where I come in. I know these people. I can help. For example, see Mrs. Higgins over there?"

She pointed to a dour-faced, older woman seated at Cutie Pies's counter. He barely glanced in her direction. He knew exactly who Mrs. Higgins was. Of course, Jessica had no way of knowing that.

Mrs. Higgins had the plump figure of an archetypal grandmother, but the sour expression of an embittered piranha. No doubt she'd been trolling the waters here at Cutie Pies for hours looking for gossip to devour.

"This isn't going to work," he said warningly.

Mrs. Higgins pressed her lips into a disapproving frown as she studied first Jessica and then Alex. Her expression hardened into grim lines when Jessica waved her over, but Alex saw the ravenous gleam in her eye and knew she was more than happy for the excuse to observe them first-hand.

"Trust me," Jessica murmured through teeth clenched behind a tight smile. "Mrs. Higgins is the president of the historical society."

Mrs. Higgins stopped beside their table, her hands

clenching the handle of her wicker shoulder bag as Jessica introduced them. Alex didn't bother to stand to shake her hand, knowing she wouldn't extend hers to him.

"Mrs. Higgins, Alex is remodeling my kitchen. He's the owner of Moreno construction."

"Hmm." She raised an eyebrow in outright speculation. "Yes, I know who Alex Moreno is."

She looked at him as if he were no better than a cockroach. One she very much wanted to squash. Under her disapproving, sanctimonious stare, he felt the remnants of his teenage rebellion stirring.

"I'm sure you do," he muttered as he stretched his legs out in front of him, slumping into the pose of a slacker as he draped his arm across the back of Jessica's chair.

He didn't take his gaze from Mrs. Higgins and did nothing to tamp down the resentment he knew simmered there. Even without glancing in Jessica's direction, he felt her stiffen and from his peripheral vision saw her shoot him a glance as she nudged him with her elbow.

Ignoring the undercurrents, Jessica plowed ahead. "Well," she said cheerfully, "then I'm sure you've heard about the great work his company did in L.A. and at the Hotel Mimosa in Marin County."

Listening to her rattle off his most recent jobs, he could barely keep himself from gaping at her in confusion. Apparently she'd looked up the references he'd included in that portfolio he'd given her that first day. She'd done her homework.

Mrs. Higgins didn't look impressed. He'd known she wouldn't be.

She sniffed loudly, finally pulling her indignant gaze from his face. Looking down her stubby nose at Jessica, she said, "Some people will hire just anyone." She turned as if to leave, then looked back over her shoulder and added, "Dear, you might want to check his references a little more closely. You'll find there are quite a few people who don't think he's up to par. Then again, maybe it isn't his skills in construction you're interested in."

As Mrs. Higgins swept from the restaurant, Alex had to clamp a hand onto Jessica's shoulder to keep her from catapulting out of her chair and storming after the woman.

"Let it go, Jess," he murmured, struggling to keep his expression blank, all too aware of the attention they'd attracted already.

"But—" she sputtered.

"Let it go."

"I've never seen her be so rude before! To imply I'd hired you just to sleep with you."

"You almost did," he pointed out. But he couldn't keep a smile from creeping onto his face. He felt absurdly pleased by her passionate defense of him.

She stiffened. "That's hardly the point. She treated you like you were slave labor or something. And not even good slave labor at that. What does she think this is, 1910?"

"Some people are just bigoted."

"Well, it's unacceptable." Suddenly she shot him a look of annoyance as she waved her hand in his direction. "And you. Don't even get me started on your behavior."

With a wince, he removed his hand from her shoulder. "My behavior?"

"Women like Mrs. Higgins put a lot of stock in propriety. You didn't even stand to shake her hand when I introduced you. Instead you just lounged there looking like some insolent delinquent."

"Trust me, I could have stood on my head to shake her hand and she wouldn't have treated me any differently."

"I don't believe that. I've known Mrs. Higgins my whole life and I've never seen her treat anyone like that. Why, I went to school with her son and—"

She broke off, a frown drifting across her face as she studied him. Her gaze open and assessing, her head slightly tilted in that way she had.

"No," she mused. "*We* went to school with her son. That's it, isn't it? Something happened between you and— What was his name?"

"Albert."

"Right. Albert." She nodded, as if remembering an important detail. "He's the one you got into that fight with right before graduation, isn't he?"

He nodded, his mind on autopilot taking him back to that day Albert—one of the boys who'd been picking on Jessica just a few weeks before—made some comment about her. Alex couldn't even remember what the comment had been now, but at the time it had made him furious.

Her frown deepened, as if she sensed there was much more he wasn't saying but wanted to. "Tell me about that day."

He shrugged and took a sip of his now-cold coffee. For the first time, he realized how coffee was like regrets, the longer you held on to them the colder and more bitter they became. "Nothing to tell. We fought. I got arrested. He didn't."

"There has to be more to it than that. Otherwise why would she still resent you?"

"Mrs. Higgins is a bigoted old fool. Sure, it doesn't help that I beat up her son, but even if that fight had never happened, to her I'd still be a dirty *mojadito*."

Jessica's expression tightened. "But that's not fair."

"Women like her never are."

She fumed for another minute before taking several deep breaths and making a visible effort to control her anger. "That's all the more reason to accept my job offer. Mrs. Higgins may be president of the historical society, but she's just one person. If you can't win her over, you'll have to work harder to convince the others you're right for the job."

Thinking back to the way she'd rattled off his last job, he asked, "What makes you so sure I am right for the job?"

She straightened, looking a little smug. "I did my research."

"Your research?"

"When you came to the house, you gave me that great portfolio about Moreno Construction. You didn't expect me not to read it, did you?"

He quirked an eyebrow. "After the way things ended that afternoon? I figured you'd just trash it."

"Well, I didn't. And after I knew what projects you'd worked on before moving back to Palo Verde, it was easy enough to poke around online a bit and get an idea of the kind of work you're capable of." She leaned forward, a spark of admiration in her eyes. "From what I read, the Hotel Mimosa was months away from being condemned. Without the work your company did, that beautiful Art Deco hotel would have been lost forever."

Alex found himself unable to tear his gaze away from hers. The awe in her eyes tugged at something deep inside him, made him feel worthy. Whole.

He forced himself to shake his head, breaking the hold her gaze seemed to have over him. "Ah, it was nothing. With a job like that, ninety percent of your success comes from finding good workers."

But she wouldn't let him off the hook. "But isn't that your job? Isn't that what makes you good at your job? Finding and managing the workers who can do quality craftsmanship at the right price? Isn't that what being a contractor is all about?"

"Mostly," he reluctantly admitted.

As she leaned back in her chair, she sent him a smug little smile that said she knew she had him exactly where she wanted him. "You know you aren't doing a very good job of selling yourself to me. You're supposed to be convincing me that being a contractor is hard work and that you are absolutely worth all the money I'm going to pay you."

"Jessica, I'm not going to let you hire me out of pity."

"It's not pity. I really want to do this. Besides, I can't recommend you unless you've worked for me," she insisted.

Or maybe he only wanted to believe she was insisting. In the end, he gave in way too easily.

She had nothing to lose except her reputation. He, on the other hand, had everything to lose. Working for Jessica could save his career or ruin it.

Losing his business worried him almost as much as losing his heart. But at least the business was still up for grabs. His heart, he feared, was already hers.

8

CONVINCING HIMSELF—not to mention his body—that he didn't want to take Jessica to bed would have been a lot easier if he didn't see her every morning. And every evening.

Every morning when he faced the intimacy of her finishing her breakfast, rinsing out her coffee mug or brushing her teeth, he swore to himself he'd be out of there long before she got home from work. Yet every evening, he hung around, filling the time with odd jobs, while he waited for the sound of her Beemer in the driveway.

Pathetic.

Not to mention stupid.

And idiotic.

And moronically pleased when she strolled through the door and said, "Oh, good, you're still here," which was what she always said when she walked in.

She always followed with some question about construction. Some new countertop material she wanted his opinion on or some question about why dovetail joints made drawers stronger.

Today, a few weeks after she'd first hired him, was no different.

"Oh, good. You're still here," she said before the front door even closed behind her. "I've got a question for you."

Setting aside the cordless drill he'd been using, he dusted off his hands. "Shoot."

"What kind of woman are you attracted to?"

"Huh?"

He'd been expecting, "What makes a better backsplash, tile or granite?" or "Could we move the stove next to the fridge?" This question he just hadn't seen coming.

"Huh?" he repeated stupidly, then added, "Um, why?"

"I've been thinking about the kind of men I usually date. Guys I've mostly met through work. But that hasn't been successful for me. Those guys have turned out to be big, boring duds. Which was the point of going out that night with Patricia."

As she spoke, she moved farther into the kitchen. She set her purse on the table and then propped her behind against the edge. With her hands braced on either side of her hips, she stretched her legs out in front of her.

"But obviously that didn't work, either," she went on. "Clearly, Paul Bunyan isn't the kind of guy I want to attract."

He tried to listen to her words, but all he could think about was her legs. She'd kicked off her shoes at the door, as she always did. Her legs were bare from the tips of her hot-pink toenail polish all the way up to where her skirt hit her midthigh.

"Maybe I shouldn't have let Patricia dress me. That must be where I went wrong."

Maybe he shouldn't have been here when she got home. That's where he went wrong.

He should have been at his house. Drinking a very big shot of Scotch. While taking a cold shower.

Maybe then he wouldn't be thinking about her legs.

Who was he kidding? He'd been fantasizing about

Jessica's legs nonstop for the past two weeks. Whether or not she was around seemed to have very little impact on how often he thought about her.

All of which might not have been so bad under other circumstances. If, for example, he knew she'd been fantasizing about him, too.

If he wouldn't ruin his career by taking her to bed and spending, oh, the next month or so with those kick-ass legs of hers wrapped around his waist.

Or if he wasn't terrified that when that month or so was up, she'd walk away and he'd be left pining for a woman he couldn't have.

Under the circumstances he had to stop acting like a lovesick boy around her. Which meant he had to get his mind off her legs and onto her conversation.

"The thing is," she was saying, "today during lunch, I was making a list of what I want in a guy. When I was done with the list, I realized, I don't want someone like Paul Bunyan or like any of the guys from work. I want someone like you."

Like him?

Or him?

His attention snapped from her legs back to her words. He searched her face, looking for answers.

A second later she realized how he'd interpreted her words. She stiffened, straightening away from the table, as a streak of red crept up her neck.

"Not you, of course. Just someone like you." She gestured emphatically.

"Right." Of course, she wasn't interested in him. Wasn't that what he'd been telling himself?

"I'm not actually hitting on you. I just—"

"I get it."

She looked away, clearly embarrassed.

His gut clenched, but not with lust. He didn't want her pity. He'd had enough pity to last him a lifetime.

Besides, it wasn't as if he was the only one affected by this attraction between them. Wiping his hands on his pants, he crossed the room to her. He didn't stop until he stood closer to her than he should.

His hands itched to touch her, but he forced his muscles to relax and his arms to hang limply by his sides. He wanted to remind her that she was just as vulnerable to this as he was.

And he needed to remind himself that he could be in the same room with her and keep his hands off her. That he still had some control where she was concerned. That this attraction—no matter how gut-wrenching—was nothing he couldn't handle and no more serious than any other mindless, sexual pull he'd ever felt.

"What was your question?" he asked, keeping his tone light, only a little curious.

"I, um…" She swallowed and he was close enough to hear the little sound her throat made when she did.

How the hell did this woman make swallowing sexy? Or maybe it was just all the things he could imagine in her mouth when she swallowed.

"Well, I was wondering—" Her hand fluttered up to her head and she tugged on a stray strand of hair.

Charmed by how flustered she seemed, he supplied, "You were wondering what kind of woman a guy like me finds attractive."

She laughed nervously. "Yes, exactly."

"Are you sure a guy like me is really what you want? You think you can handle a guy like me?"

Her laughter faded and again she swallowed hard. He wanted nothing more than to run his mouth down the length of her neck and trace those contracting muscles with his tongue.

"No," she admitted. "I'm not."

"The problem is, Jess, you take everything so seriously."

She nodded and he imagined she swayed toward him. "Yes," she breathed. "I mean, I do. But—"

"And guys like me, well, we don't take anything seriously at all."

"Well, you see—"

"Guys like me like to keep things light. Fun."

"Light and fun," she repeated as if making a mental list.

"Casual," he explained. "Playful. Maybe even a little wild."

"Got it. Casual and playful. Maybe wild."

Despite the fact that her mere nearness had his blood pressure skyrocketing off the charts, he couldn't help smiling.

"What?" she demanded, eyeing him suspiciously.

"Nothing."

"You're laughing at me."

He shook his head, but said, "Yes, I am." Then he couldn't keep it down any longer and he chuckled. "You look like you're itching to take notes."

"I don't know what you mean."

But she did. He could see it in her eyes. "You want to take notes. You want to brainstorm ideas of how to achieve 'fun' and 'playful' and then write them down in that Day-Timer you're always carting around."

She fidgeted, her gaze skittering nervously away from his, so that he knew he'd nailed it.

As soon as the phrase "nailed it" slipped into his mind, he thought instantly of what else he'd like to nail. Or rather, who.

God, he wanted her.

And before he knew it, he was touching her. Just running his knuckle down her cheek in a whisper-soft touch that left him aching for more. The way she arched into his caress didn't help matters. The way her eyelids drifted closed, as if she'd been hypnotized and was completely at his mercy.

As if he wasn't having a hard enough time keeping his hands off her as it was. As if he wasn't already aching to take her to bed, where it'd be far more complicated than plain ol' ordinary sex. Plain ol' ordinary mind-blowing sex.

Way to keep it light and casual.

He should have known that would come back to bite him in the ass.

She had to know how much he wanted her. But with any luck, he could keep her from knowing that his feelings for her were anything but casual.

"Come on, Jess," he murmured. "You know you're dying to do it."

Her breath caught and her eyes fluttered open. "Do what?"

"Make a list. Analyze how to be fun and playful."

Only when she recoiled slightly from his touch did he realize there was a hint of challenge in his voice.

For a second he thought she was going to back down. Or be offended. Instead her eyes lit up in response to the challenge.

"I can be fun and playful."

"Yeah, right."

"You think I can't be fun and playful? Because I can *be* fun and playful."

"Sure you can, princess."

"I can!" she insisted.

"Tell me one thing you've done that's fun and playful, let alone wild."

She opened her mouth then an instant later snapped it closed. Her lips pursed and her forehead furrowed. After a long moment she said, "I went out to the club with Patricia. That was fun. I let you do body shots off my neck. That was wild."

"Don't forget. I was there."

"So?"

"So, I know how much you hated being in that club. And that body shot you did was the most ladylike, least-wild body shot I've ever seen."

It had also been sexy enough to nearly blow the top of his head off, but she didn't need to know that. The pathetic truth was, if Jessica ever did shed that pristine, princess facade of hers and get really wild, he'd be in serious trouble.

"But—"

"That body shot may have been wild for you, but by most standards, that was tame. Some body shots are poured straight onto a woman's naked belly."

He trailed a finger down the outside of her sweater to her stomach. He heard her quick intake of breath, felt the quiver of her contracting muscles.

"The tequila runs across her belly, pooling in her navel. You have to run your tongue all over to get it. It's sticky and messy and very, very hot."

And just the thought of doing that to Jessica—of running his tongue all over her—made his blood pound. But worse than his own reaction was watching hers.

Her breath was coming fast and shallow now. Her eyelids at half-mast, her body swaying toward him. All he had to do was touch her and she'd dissolve into his arms.

Just a single touch and she'd be his.

"Alex, I—"

He shook his head, not giving her the chance to finish her sentence. If she was going to beg him to take her to bed, he couldn't bear to hear it. "Sorry, Jess. You're just not going to convince me you're the type who likes it messy."

But if they ever had sex, that's how he'd want her. Hot, sweating and begging. And very, very messy.

Yeah, right. As if that was ever going to happen.

"You're just not the type," he said.

His words seemed to snap her out of her stupor and irritation flashed in her eyes. "You don't know that," she protested.

"Sure I do. You've got 'good girl' written all over you. Everything from your sensible shoes to the conservative clothes to the way you wear your hair."

She looked down at her clothes, as if to ascertain what was wrong with them. "You don't like the way I dress?"

He loved the way she dressed. So tailored, so conservative. So unswervingly prim and proper. Yesterday it had been a navy pantsuit. Today, slim black pants and a pale pink sweater set.

And as always she looked incredibly classy. Undeniably rich.

Everything about her appearance should have reminded him how out of his reach she was. Instead, her outward appearance only reminded him of the passions that lurked beneath her prim-and-proper surface. Passions that nearly boiled over every time he touched her.

All the more reason not to touch her.

Reminding himself not to touch Jessica was becoming a full-time job. One that would be a hell of a lot easier if she'd leave him in peace.

Hoping to placate her and to end the conversation, he said, "Hey, there's nothing wrong with the way you dress."

She didn't look placated. Frowning, she looked down at her clothes. "Nothing wrong except that you don't like it."

"I didn't say that," he pointed out.

"You didn't have to." Her frown deepened as she plucked at the hem of her sweater. "You don't like my sweater set." She shrugged out of the button-up sweater and tossed it onto the kitchen chair. Extending her arms to show off the tank she wore underneath, she asked, "Better?"

With her shoulders bare and the bulky top sweater removed, she looked unbelievably appealing. Her sweater tank fit snug across her breasts and clung to her narrow waist, yet somehow it was her bare arms he couldn't pull his eyes away from. Her upper arms were smooth and tanned, her shoulders gently curved. And the strap of her bra peeked out from beneath her sweater, a swatch of dark purple nestled against a faint sprinkling of freckles.

From just that glimpse of purple his mind filled in a thousand details. Her bra would be one those little half push-ups jobs. The kind that cupped a woman's breasts and offered them to a man like the most decadent of treats. Satin and lace, but cut down almost to her nipples.

Knowing Jessica, she'd have matching panties. They'd be cut high over her thighs or maybe even—God help him—a thong.

He swallowed the groan he felt threatening to escape, but he couldn't manage to banish the image.

"What?" Jessica asked. "Is it really that bad?"

"Huh?" was all he could mutter.

"You hate it, don't you? You hate the way I dress."

"No," he said too quickly. "I just…"

But what the hell could he say without sounding like a pervert? *I was just picturing you in a thong, could you repeat the question?*

"Hate the way I dress," she finished for him. "And why wouldn't you? I dress like my mother. I dress like a spinster."

"A what?"

"An old maid. So will you help me or not?"

"Help you do what?" Had he missed part of the conversation when he was fantasizing about Jessica wearing a thong? Because he had no idea what she was talking about.

"Go shopping. Will you help me pick out new clothes?"

Shopping? For clothes? What a nightmare. "Why would I do that?" He tried to keep the horror from his voice, but wasn't sure he managed it.

She looked a little hurt, but after a minute she said, "Okay, then. I guess I'll go alone."

Thank God.

"I haven't been to that new Galleria in Roseville." She cocked her head to the side in that cute way she did when she was thinking about something. "I'm pretty sure they've got a Victoria's Secret."

Victoria's Secret? Ah, crap.

With an expression of guileless innocence, she added, "You know, I've never even been in a Victoria's Secret. Not even once."

Thank God. That meant the bra strap he'd glimpsed wasn't part of some mind-blowingly sexy getup. He could stop torturing himself imagining it.

Then she smiled gamely. "Well, there's a first time for everything."

He did not need to know that.

Again the image of her in nothing but a dark purple bra and thong flashed through his mind. He ruthlessly shoved the image to the deepest corner of his troubled psyche.

Okay, this wasn't too bad. As long as he didn't have to see her wearing anything from Victoria's Secret, he could handle it. Besides, he was already picturing her in her lingerie anyway. It couldn't get much worse than this, right?

But then it did.

"I wonder," she mused. "Do you think the Victoria's Secret stores sell clothes like the catalogs do? I've always wanted to wear clothes like that."

"You have?"

"Sure. All those short little skirts and cute little shirts." He must have looked worried, because she hastened to reassure him, "That's not to say I won't shop for lingerie, too, of course. If I'm lucky, I can buy everything I need there. What do you think?"

What did he think? He was a dead man, that's what he thought. She was going to go shopping and come back dressed like his hottest, wildest fantasy.

There was no way in hell he could let her shop alone.

"Okay, we'll go shopping. But there's no way—no way in hell—I'm going in to Victoria's Secret."

She smiled brightly. "Okay."

He just stared at her for a minute while a feeling of dread sunk in. How the hell had she gotten him to agree to go shopping with her? And why did he feel as if he'd been manipulated by a master?

9

YESTERDAY, Alex had teased her about the lists she kept in her Day-Timer. Oh, if only he knew…

Her Day-Timer was now devoted almost entirely to Operation Be Saucy, which somehow had shifted focus from The List to her plans to seduce Alex.

Career goals had fallen away in favor of lists of seductive skills she wished to master. Tips she'd gleaned from *Cosmo* now filled the pages where business appointments had previously been listed. And on the very first page was her Priority Action sheet on which she'd written the characteristics he wanted most in a woman. Fun, casual, light, playful and wild.

And if that's what Alex found sexy, then by golly, that was what she would be.

Saturday morning, as she dressed for their shopping trip in tailored shorts and a snug-fitted T-shirt, she felt like a general preparing for war.

Armed with knowledge and determination, she marched into battle.

She would get him into bed. She would get her passionate fling. If for no other reason than to prove to herself just how saucy she could be.

And whenever doubts arose within her that there might be another reason for wanting to sleep with Alex, she squashed them ruthlessly.

Of course, actually getting him to the mall had been challenging, and if the way he was dragging his feet was any indication, it might take quite a bit of manipulation to get his honest opinion on clothes.

"What about this store?" he asked as they made their way through the mall.

She looked in the direction he pointed, then shook her head in frustration. He'd been making stupid suggestions like this all morning. "That store sells purses and belts."

"So?"

"You can't seriously want to help me shop for accessories." She slowed her pace to let a pack of noisy teenagers drift past. Once they were out of earshot, she leaned in closer and whispered, "But if it's leather you're interested in—"

Before she could finish the thought, he gripped her elbow and propelled her past the store. His expression taut and unyielding, he muttered, "Forget it."

"You don't like leather?" she asked innocently. The possessiveness of his hand on her arm thrilled her, sending little fissures of pleasure racing through her body and giving her the courage to be bold. "Because it is kind of wild."

"I said forget it."

"I'm just trying to be open-minded."

The hand on her elbow tightened convulsively then loosened. Instantly she missed his touch and the loss only renewed her determination.

A short while later, when Alex was pulling another one of his what-about-this? tricks—this time outside a store that sold hiking boots—she spotted it.

There, in the window of one of the trendy boutiques, was the perfect outfit. The skirt was short, but not tight like the one Patricia had picked out. Instead it fell in soft waves

NO POSTAGE
NECESSARY
IF MAILED
IN THE
UNITED STATES

BUSINESS REPLY MAIL
FIRST-CLASS MAIL   PERMIT NO. 717-003   BUFFALO, NY

POSTAGE WILL BE PAID BY ADDRESSEE

HARLEQUIN READER SERVICE
3010 WALDEN AVE
PO BOX 1867
BUFFALO NY 14240-9952

PLAY THE
Lucky Key Game

Do You Have the LUCKY KEY?

and you can get

FREE BOOKS
and a **FREE GIFT!**

Scratch the gold areas with a coin. Then check below to see the books and gift you can get!

YES!
I have scratched off the gold areas. Please send me the **2 FREE BOOKS** and **GIFT** for which I qualify. I understand I am under no obligation to purchase any books, as explained on the back of this card.

350 HDL D399   150 HDL D4AN

FIRST NAME   LAST NAME

ADDRESS

APT.#   CITY

STATE/PROV.   ZIP/POSTAL CODE

2 free books plus a free gift   1 free book

2 free books   Try Again!

around the thighs of the mannequin, its pale floral print the perfect counterpoint to the sweater paired with it. The cornflower-blue sweater tank was miles away from the shell she'd worn just the night before. The knit was just loose enough to reveal glimpses of skin beneath. It scooped low in front and in back. The store had paired it with comfy, low-slung sandals, a chunky string of beads and a floppy woven hat. Now that was a playful outfit.

It was beautiful and feminine. She'd usually avoided floral prints. They seemed to require a delicate femininity that she'd never quite mastered.

But she could see herself wearing it. In fact, she yearned to rush into the store to try it on.

But what would Alex say?

She glanced in his direction. His face registered a look of horror. Either he hated the outfit or he loved it. But which?

"What do you think?"

He swallowed. "I, um… It's a little small, isn't it?"

He loved it. Definitely.

"Come on, I'll try it on, then you can decide if it's too small." She grabbed his hand and pulled him toward the entrance.

Yanking stubbornly against her hand, he protested. "What about that store?" He pointed across the fairway. "Those clothes look bigger."

She glanced toward the store in question, then sighed in exasperation. "Of course those clothes are bigger. Those are maternity clothes."

"Oh. Right."

She took advantage of his momentary shock and dragged him the rest of the way into the store. Ten minutes later, she shucked her Princess Jessica attire and slipped into the flirty little skirt.

The second she walked out of the dressing room and saw Alex's expression, she knew this outfit would drive him crazy. This outfit would wear him down.

He'd been sprawled in the chair, his long, denim-clad legs stretched out in front of him, his knees apart, his shoulders slumped as he chewed mindlessly on a toothpick.

The instant he saw her, he stilled. To an observer, he might have seemed relaxed. Bored even. However, she felt the energy coming off him in waves. His expression as he watched her—so studied and intense—was as erotic as if he'd crossed the room and begun to undress her. His gaze traveled down the length of her throat. It skimmed over the crests of her breasts, just barely visible above the scooped neckline of the sweater, down the skirt, to where the hemline ended midthigh. Then his eyes stopped and he just stared at her bare legs.

She shivered under the intensity of his gaze and had to look away. Nervously, she scanned the store, sure that the tension between them was attracting attention. But as she glanced around, the store seemed empty.

Tucked into the back corner of the store, with towers of clothes shielding them from view, they were virtually alone. With that thought, a kind of reckless confidence propelled her toward him.

As she approached his chair, he straightened. With that toothpick clenched tightly between his teeth, he looked tense enough to bolt. Stopping just between his outstretched feet, she twirled around so the skirt belled around her legs. Peering at him from over her shoulder she asked, "What do you think?"

He swallowed, then pulled the toothpick from between his teeth and tossed it into the wastebasket by the chair. "It's short."

Pretending she hadn't quite heard him, she moved closer, perching on the arm of his chair, stretching her legs beside his. "Yes, but do you like it?"

He stiffened, but didn't move away from her. So she crossed her legs, and running one foot up the back of his calf, she pressed, "Is it sexy?"

He all but jumped out of the chair to get away from her. "You know what's sexy? Long skirts."

"Long skirts?" she asked seriously, trying her best to hide her triumphant amusement.

"Yep. Long skirts." He pulled something off a nearby rack and thrust it at her. "Long skirts and bulky sweaters. And layers. Lots of layers."

As he spoke he pushed first one piece of clothing and then another into her hands. Within seconds, she had a chest-high stack of clothes, none of which matched, most of it the wrong size.

She dropped the clothes into the chair he'd abandoned and crossed to where he was holding up an oatmeal-colored fishermen's sweater easily big enough for him to wear. She moved in close so that only the width of the sweater separated them. It was a bulky sweater, but not that bulky, and she could feel the effect she had on him.

Knowing she'd turned him on—in public, for goodness' sake—nearly drove her crazy. "You don't really find this sweater sexy, do you?"

"Sure I do," he replied too quickly.

"It's big," she pointed out.

"That's what's sexy about it."

He was grasping at straws now. He had no idea what he was talking about. And she'd bet he hadn't even glanced at the sweater in question. Well, that was fine by her.

"I suppose," she said innocently, "that you're going to tell me that this sweater is sexy not because of how much it reveals but because of how much it hides."

"Sure."

"Because when a woman's wearing a sweater like this, the man has no idea what she's wearing underneath."

"Right. Exactly." But he sounded a little less sure now, anticipating her next words.

"Sure, maybe she's wearing a plain white cotton bra and panties." At the word "panties," his gaze darkened and her pulse kicked up a notch in response. "But maybe not." She could hardly believe how bold he made her feel. "Maybe she's wearing some sexy little lingerie set she picked out when you weren't watching. Or maybe she's wearing nothing at all."

"Nothing?" His voice sounded strained to the limit.

She nodded, smiling. "That's one of the things on the list."

His gaze darkened and he swallowed visibly. She felt an intoxicating surge of feminine power as he lowered his head as if to kiss her, but she stepped back before he could.

Keeping her tone light, despite the trembling need she tried to hide, she folded the sweater and said, "You're right, I think I will buy this sweater. Good choice."

It took all her control to walk away from him when—frankly—she would have preferred to pull him into the dressing room with her and have her way with him.

He might even have been agreeable to a little tryst in the dressing room, but she wanted more than that. She wanted him all to herself and she wanted all night long. No distractions, no complications, just the two of them.

And he wanted it, too. He just didn't want to admit it.

10

SOMETIMES A MAN should know when to keep his mouth shut. It was a skill Alex had never quite mastered.

Apparently the other day when he'd told Jessica he liked playful women, she'd taken it as a personal challenge. Big shock there. Now, as he packed up his tools after a long day tearing out her upper kitchen cabinets, she was treating him to a lengthy diatribe about all the fun and playful things she'd done in the past year.

"I didn't—"

He shook his head ruefully, cutting her off. "Whether you're fun and playful or not, being in the bar wasn't fun for you."

"But—"

"And that body shot definitely wasn't playful." To make matters worse, she was wearing the sweater he'd picked out. The damn thing was driving him crazy. Just as she'd predicted, he couldn't stop wondering what she had on underneath it. "You did that only because you hate to back down from a challenge."

"That's not true."

"Come on, Jess. I was there. If you hadn't been backed into a corner, there's no way you would have let me do that body shot."

She frowned. "So what you're saying is that men like

you are attracted to women who do that kind of thing. To women who do body shots in bars?"

Before Jessica? No, he hadn't been. But since that night? Hell, since then, all he could think about was how she'd looked perched on the edge of that bar. How her body had felt beneath his hands and how her skin had tasted. That was, when he wasn't wondering what she had on under that freakin' sweater.

All of which he knew he should damn well keep to himself. But he didn't. He was tired of her pushing his buttons. Tired of keeping his mouth shut. And before his common sense could kick in, the instincts he'd been suppressing for weeks now flared to life and took over.

"Am I attracted to women who do body shots in bars? No, not really." Relief flickered across her face, until he kept talking. "But if I'm going to drink tequila at all, I'd rather drink it off a woman's skin, not out of a glass." Her eyes widened at his words. And he couldn't help noticing how the color darkened, making them an even deeper blue. "I won't lie to you, Jess, ever since having you up on that bar that Friday night, I've been thinking about getting you up there again."

She opened her mouth to speak, but this time he was the one who stopped her.

"But I've never been much of an exhibitionist. So next time, it wouldn't be in a bar, it'd be private and preferably close to a bed. Just the two of us."

He was standing so close to her he could see every flicker of emotion that crossed her face. He saw the many layers of her heated response. The interest. The desire. The anticipation. Even the flicker of trepidation.

He saw her struggle to bring her reaction under control, but took pleasure in knowing it was no easier for her than it was for him.

She may want him, but he didn't doubt for a minute that all her desire was tied back to the damn list. For her, he was convenient. She wanted a passionate fling and thought he could give it to her.

To make matters worse, she was totally focused on the "passionate" part of passionate fling. But all he could think about was the "fling."

Flings, passionate or not, were short-lived. A week, maybe two, if he was lucky. But he wanted so much more from her than that.

He chuckled at the irony. "Maybe you're right. Maybe you could handle fun and playful just fine. Maybe it's the pure, gut-wrenching lust you've got a problem with."

He didn't know why he'd said it. Maybe hoping to scare her off. But he'd forgotten that nothing scared Jessica.

To his amazement, she didn't even look away. "Maybe you're right. Maybe that's part of the problem." Her nervous laughter told him she wasn't as unflappable as she appeared. "Maybe I do keep my distance from—as you put it—the pure, gut-wrenching lust. Or maybe the problem is that men always assume women like me just aren't interested in the pure, gut-wrenching lust."

This time, he was the one to back away. It was just a half step and not nearly enough distance to give him back his perspective, but just enough to keep him from reaching out to her.

It did not, however, keep her from closing the space between them. In an instant she was standing so close that her body was almost plastered against his. Her hand was hot on his arm as her lips tilted up to him.

Suddenly all the reasons why he shouldn't kiss her vanished. All the arguments against getting involved with her that had been running through his head for weeks now just disappeared. The only thing he could think about was how sweet and hot she'd taste and how good she smelled and how he wanted more than anything to touch her. And to keep on touching her.

He might have had the strength to resist her, but before he could muster any of that strength, she pressed her body to his. With one hand in his hair, she pulled his head down to hers and she strained onto her toes to kiss him.

The kiss was hot and deep. Pure gut-wrenching lust.

He tried to back away from her, but she followed him step for step until he felt the counter at his back. Only then did he give in completely, opening his mouth to her persistence. As soon as he felt her tongue dart between his lips and the sweet suction of her kiss, he knew he was a goner.

Why had he even been fighting it?

He ran his hands down the length of her, reveling in the feel of her soft curves beneath the bulk of her sweater. A sweater that looked demure, but didn't hide the heart-stopping body beneath.

Besides, he knew the truth about Jessica.

For all she seemed like the perfect good girl, that was an act. Just beneath the surface lurked a fun and passionate woman who'd never be light and casual.

He only hoped she didn't see beneath his surface as easily as he saw beneath hers. Because she'd know that he didn't want light and casual. He only wanted her.

He wanted more than a passionate fling. He wanted more than just her body. He wanted her heart and her soul. And he wanted them forever.

ALEX WAS WRONG. This wasn't pure gut-wrenching lust. It was pure heaven.

Never before had a simple kiss made her ache with

need. Never before had the feel of a man's hands on her hips made her weak in the knees. Made her ears ring, for goodness' sake.

At least, she thought it was his kiss that made her feel that way. But maybe she was weak in the knees because she'd missed lunch. Maybe the ringing in her ears was just…

Just his cell phone.

She released her hold on him and tried to step away. He didn't let her go, but lifted his head and stared at her for a heartbeat, his eyes glazed with passion.

"Your phone," she said numbly, trying again to step back.

"Let it go."

Before he could lower his mouth to hers again, she pressed her palm against his chest and stopped him. "That's your work phone. You should answer it."

He looked ready to argue with her, but instead he yanked the phone from his hip and jabbed the button. "Moreno here."

Wanting to give him privacy for the phone call, she tried to pull away, but he kept his arm anchored firmly across her shoulders. Cradled against his chest, with the strength of his arm holding her firmly against him, she could only rest her head against his shoulder and relax.

At least she tried to relax. Tried to calm herself and her reaction to him. But she was all too aware of the tensing muscles of his chest and the thudding of his heartbeat beneath her hand. More than anything, she was aware of her own reaction to him.

Of the heat slowly burning its way through her. Of the heavy weight of her breasts and the need she felt to press them against his chest, as if that could ease the desire driving her wild.

She tried to ignore the half of the conversation she could

hear, but she caught a word or two. The name of a street not far from her house. The name Veronica. Information that barely registered in her mind before being helplessly dislodged when he slipped his foot between hers.

Her legs automatically parted, allowing his thigh to slide up to the juncture between her legs. Squeezing her eyes closed, she concentrated on not moving, even though her every instinct urged her to rock her hips forward, to rub herself against him, to ease the heaviness building inside of her.

His arm tightened across her back as the muscles beneath her hands tensed. She sensed him struggling for control and that only made it harder on her. She felt as if her skin were on fire and the only way to extinguish that fire was to touch Alex. To pull his shirt from the waistband of his jeans and to rub her palms over the muscles of his chest. To rid herself of her clothes and to rub her skin against his. To rip the phone from his hand, toss it aside and have her way with him this instant.

But she couldn't do that.

Enough of his conversation made it through the fog of her desire for her to realize this was most definitely not a personal call. This Veronica wanted him to come by to give her an estimate. And—unless she was mistaken— he'd just agreed to be there within the hour.

Tapping down an irrational surge of jealousy, Jessica tried to muster up some happiness for him. He didn't need to tell her what this next job could mean for his business. He'd mentioned more than once how much trouble he was having finding work.

And she knew how important making his business a success was to him. Until he did, he'd never really believe he was good enough.

With a sigh, she let her head drop back to his shoulder,

her aching need for him cooling with the realization that—whatever else happened tonight—she would not be ripping the phone from his hands, tearing his clothes from his body and having her way with him.

At least not tonight. And maybe not ever.

A few seconds later he ended his call and tossed the phone aside. Since the last thing she wanted was to listen to him make excuses about why he couldn't stay, she beat him to the punch.

"I know. You have to go."

He squeezed her shoulder again, resettling her against his body. "Thanks."

"For what?"

"For understanding."

Funny, she didn't feel understanding. She felt frustrated and annoyed. Mad at herself for wanting more than he could give and mad at him for not being able to give it.

Not wanting to sound as irrational as she felt, she still couldn't keep herself from muttering, "Why does this have to be so hard?"

He chuckled. "You want a scientific explanation?"

With the length of his erection nuzzled against her hip, she had no trouble interpreting his innuendo. A strangled laugh escaped her lips. "That's not what I meant."

"I know."

She felt his sigh ruffle the hair at her temple. This time, when she pulled away, he let her go. A few shuffling, backward steps later, she propped her hips on the opposite counter.

Even though several feet now separated them, her body still trembled with need and she felt the heat of his gaze on her skin as potently as she'd felt his touch.

"Look, I know your business is the most important

thing in your life right now. And I know you think getting involved with me will be bad for your business…"

She let her words trail off, watching him carefully to gauge his response.

Deny it, she thought. *Contradict me. Tell me I'm wrong. Tell me I'm crazy.*

But he offered her no reassurances. Instead, he met her gaze with a steady silence that spoke more loudly than words could. As far as he was concerned, a relationship between the two of them was still out of the question.

Not that she wanted to be more important to him than his business.

If this was just a fling, then she certainly couldn't expect to be the center of his universe. She couldn't expect him to make sacrifices for her.

And this *was* just a fling. Short term. No emotional commitment. Very *Saucy*.

That's what she wanted. Wasn't it?

Pushing her confusion and doubts aside, she said, "So, tell me about this job."

He hesitated, then said, "It's just down the street from you. A neighbor who saw the sign I put in your front yard, actually."

"But what kind of job is it?" she pressed. "A remodel? An addition? What?"

Instead of answering right away, he turned his back to her and started gathering up his tools. "Sort of an addition."

"'Sort of an addition'? What's that supposed to mean?"

"They want to add on an outdoor living space."

He loaded up the rest of his tools without once meeting her gaze. He was dissembling, which just wasn't like him. So she kept pushing. "An outdoor living space? Do you mean a sunroom?"

"No, not a sunroom. More of a—" He winced. "A deck."

"A deck?"

The tinge of red in his cheeks told her he was embarrassed—maybe even ashamed—by the job. And just like that, the intimacy between them evaporated. Damn, she should really learn to bite her tongue.

Torn between wishing she could take back the words and wanting to make him understand her meaning, she said, "Alex, you're a general contractor. I wouldn't have thought building decks was the kind of job you did."

His jaw tightened, a sure sign he thought she was overstepping some boundaries. "It's a job."

"Sure, it's a job, but I've seen the work you're capable of. You should be remodeling historic buildings, not building decks."

"I'm not in a position where I can turn down work."

"And if you get a reputation for building decks and fences, instead of remodels and construction, you never will be."

"I can't be that picky. It's good, honest work. There's nothing wrong doing manual labor."

"Well, sure." Her voice rose with the heat of the argument. "If that's your job, but you can do more than that."

"My parents do manual labor. They have for over thirty years now. It's how they put food on the table."

Great. And now she'd inadvertently insulted his family.

Resisting the urge to bury her face and groan, she said, "I'm sorry. I didn't mean—"

But he didn't give her the chance to backpedal. "I'm not ashamed of the way they made a living. And I'm not too proud to do the work they did."

His voice was thick with emotion. Emotions more complicated than just his anger of her inadvertent slip.

Maybe he actually was *ashamed of how they'd made their living*.

Feeling a bit like she was approaching a wounded bear, she crossed to him and placed a hand on his arm. She spoke with a soft voice, determined to make him understand. "I truly didn't mean to insult your parents."

He looked up at her, studying her for a long minute before nodding.

"There isn't anything wrong with doing manual labor. I admire the people who make their living that way. They work harder than I do, for less money. You're right to be proud of the work your parents did. But there's nothing wrong with wanting more than that."

She wanted him to know that she understood his mixed emotions, even if he didn't understand them himself. "Besides, you told me yourself that your parents wanted a different life for you. How do you think they'd feel knowing you were thinking of wasting your time on a job like this?"

For a second she thought she might have swayed him, but then he looked away from her and pulled his arm out from under her hand. "It's not wasted time if I'm paid for the work."

"But—"

"I'll be doing that job over the weekends." He unplugged an extension cord and began to loop it from his hand to his elbow. "You don't have to worry that it'll take time away from this project."

He was being so stubborn it made her want to howl with frustration. "You know that's not what I'm worried about. I couldn't care less when you finish this job. But what about your bid for the renovations on the county courthouse? If you're spending all your time building decks, when are you going to work on that?" He said nothing, but the grim set of his jaw told her everything she needed to know. "Oh, I see. You're not going to work up a bid for the courthouse, are you?"

"I didn't say that."

"You didn't have to." Shaking her head, she turned to leave the kitchen, only to spin back to face him a few steps later, unable to leave it alone. "I can't believe you let that woman bully you like this."

"If you're talking about Mrs. Higgins, I didn't let her—"

"Excuse me, but that's exactly what you did. The last time we talked about it, you were still planning on turning in a bid. You weren't optimistic, but you were going to do it. But all it took was a few thinly veiled insults from that meddling old cow and all of sudden you back down?"

"That meddling old cow—as you put it—has the power to veto any bid I turn in. I'm not going to waste my time working up a bid I know I don't have a shot at winning."

"So what are you going to do instead? Waste your time building decks?"

"It's a job," he repeated, his voice strained and slow, a sure sign he was as tired of this argument as she was.

But she still couldn't let it go. Not when she *knew* she was right.

"Sure it's a job, but it's a job that's beneath you. Look, don't get me wrong, there's nothing wrong with building decks or doing manual labor, but you are capable of so much more." She gestured to the work he'd done in her kitchen. "I've seen the work you can do."

He frowned. "How—"

"I went online and downloaded the before-and-after

pictures of the hotel you worked on in Marin County," she admitted, waving aside his question, hoping to move on quickly so that admission didn't make her sound like a stalker. "You did amazing work on that hotel. But then, it wasn't just you doing the work, was it? You admitted you had a whole crew working on that project. Not to mention subcontractors. Having that kind of job in your portfolio should have made your career."

Though there was a glint in his eyes warning her she was pushing too hard, he said nothing. The look itself almost stopped her. But she'd already angered him. What harm would it do to finish proving her point?

"But instead of parlaying that success into another career-defining job, you decided to move back here. Ostensibly to prove to the people of this town that you've changed."

That—finally—got a rise out him. "'Ostensibly'?"

But she ignored him and went on. "That you've made something of yourself. But that isn't what you've done. Instead of going after the one job that will prove exactly that, you're satisfied with remodeling kitchens and building decks."

"'Ostensibly?'" he repeated, his tone rising in irritation.

"Yes, ostensibly. You don't seriously think you're going to impress anyone building decks, do you? If you really want to show these people what you're capable of, you have to get that job remodeling the courthouse. You have to—"

This time, he cut her off, crossing to her in a few short steps and wrapping his hands around her upper arms. "You think I don't want this job? You think I haven't thought of this?" He tugged her closer, so that they were almost touching. "I *have* thought about it. Of course I want this job. But since I moved back here, it's been obvious there are some things I just can't have." He sucked in a deep breath. "Sometimes you just have to let it go."

And just like that, he released his hold on her.

Before he stepped away, she reached for him. "Sometimes you have to fight for what you want. You can't settle for what people are willing to give you. You can't just give up."

"I'm not giving up. I've still got work."

"But you're the best person for that job. You know you are. You can't settle for any less than you deserve. You just can't. Besides, if you're satisfied with whatever crappy and demeaning jobs the people in the town deign to throw your way, then the only thing you're proving to them is that they were right about you. That you really are good for nothing. Nothing important at least."

He jerked his hand out from hers. "I need to go. If I'm late, I won't get the job. Then it won't matter whether or not you think it's beneath me."

As he turned away from her, she saw that his gaze was dark and shuttered. His expression completely closed.

Dang it, why did she always manage to say the wrong thing around him?

"Alex, I didn't mean—"

She reached out to him again, but he neatly avoided her touch and cut her off at the same time. "What does it matter to you, anyway? What difference could it possibly make to you what this town thinks of me? Surely you're not worried about my reputation rubbing off on yours? Because that was the idea all along, wasn't it? That being with me would bring you down to earth a little bit. That sleeping with me would show people how wild you really are. Hell, I'd think the fact I'm a manual laborer would only enhance that."

"I just thought—"

"What? That because we kissed you had the right to stick your nose into my personal business? Well, you were wrong. That was just about sex, Jess. Nothing more."

"But—"

"See, that's exactly what I meant."

"Meant?" she asked numbly.

"About you. You take everything much too seriously, princess. You just don't know when to keep things light and casual."

11

THE FIGHT with Alex left Jessica in a sour mood. She'd told herself all along that all she wanted from Alex was a few nights of passion. And last night she'd nearly had it. She had nearly worn him down. If it hadn't been for that dang phone call, she might now be basking in some serious afterglow. Instead they'd fought.

If anything, she should be upset that her plans to seduce Alex had once again gone astray. Instead, it was the fight that nagged at her. He'd all but told her to butt out of his life.

Why did that bother her? She'd been telling herself all she wanted from Alex was a few nights of passion.

He'd made it clear he wanted nothing more from her than a light, fun fling. Which was all she really needed to check number one off The List. So why did she suddenly feel sick to her stomach?

She tried to bury her doubts while at work, tried to mask her fears. And she might have managed to do it, if she hadn't stopped by the break room to check her mail and run into Peter—Handheld Technologies's resident lothario.

She normally managed to avoid Peter altogether, since he worked in the marketing department. He'd also never before sought her out, which was fine by her—especially if even a fraction of the sleazy rumors were true.

But today, Peter's gaze skimmed the length of her body suggestively before returning to her face. "Hi."

She made a nonsensical comment on the weather while feigning interest in a United Way donation request, then headed for the door. She almost made it before he stopped her.

"Jessica, hold up a minute."

You've got to be kidding. Letting disdain drip from her voice, she said merely, "Yes?"

"I..." He smiled broadly at her, but clearly had to search for a topic of conversation. "I've been having some problems with the Carson account."

Assessing him through narrowed eyes, she looked for any hint of what he really wanted. Surely he wasn't going to hit on her. "I haven't worked on the Carson account in over three months," she said pointedly. "I was taken off the team when I went to Sweden. I can't possibly be any help."

"Right." He nodded, obviously looking for an excuse to keep her here. "Well, sure, but...you're so good, I bet you remember all about the account." He slanted her a greasy smile. "You probably still have some great insights. Have you eaten yet? Maybe we could talk about it over lunch."

"It's three-thirty. So, yeah, I've eaten lunch." She turned to leave, but he fell into step beside her as she made her way to her office.

"What about dinner?"

"What about you leaving me alone?"

He stopped her, grabbing her arm so she had to turn and face him. "Come on, Jessica, you can drop that good-little-girl charade you've got going." He ran his hand up and down her arm in a way he no doubt thought was provocative. "You don't have to pretend with me."

She shook his hand off her arm. "Pretend?"

"To be all prim and proper."

"I don't know what you're talking about." Her tone still dripping with disdain, she could only hope it hid her trepidation. She was afraid she knew exactly what he was talking about.

"You and Alex Moreno. Oh, come on, Jessica, surely you didn't think people wouldn't find out."

"There is nothing going on between Alex and me." Not that she hadn't been trying. "We're just friends."

"Don't be naive." The hard note of cynicism in his voice grated her nerves. "Guys like Alex aren't *friends* with women."

"What do you mean, guys like Alex? You don't even know him."

"I know all about him. I've heard all about his wild past, picking fights and getting into trouble. Causing—"

"That was in the past. He's grown up now. He's an adult. A concept you, apparently, haven't grasped."

"Keep telling yourself that."

"What's that supposed to mean?"

Peter shrugged but there was no hiding the insulting implication in his gaze. "It just seems to me that if a guy like that is fooling around with you, he must be doing it just to prove he can. It must be quite a thrill for someone like him to knock a prissy little good girl like you off her pedestal."

For a moment she merely floundered in her indignation. Finally she narrowed her eyes to a glare and stepped closer to him. "What bothers you, Peter? The fact that I'm slumming? Or the fact that I didn't come to you to go slumming?" As he stood there gaping mutely at her, she raked him with a dismissive stare. "I decided that if I was going to climb down off my pedestal, I wanted to do it with a real man."

Then she turned on her heel, walked the rest of the way to her office and waltzed inside before closing the door with a simple click. The second the door shut behind her, she sank against it.

What a mess. What a nasty, icky mess.

Of course, she'd always known Peter was a jerk, but today he'd sunk below even her expectations of him.

But that was the least of her worries. Peter may be a jerk, but what if he was right? After all, there was a certain logic to that. Alex had told her over and over again that she wasn't his type. What if Alex was attracted to her just because of the thrill of—what was the phrase Peter had used?—knocking a "prissy little good girl" like her off her pedestal?

Worse still, Peter's accusations actually hurt. A sign she was way more emotionally involved than she'd ever meant to be. A sign she might even be falling—

No. She was *not* falling in love with Alex.

Saucy women did not fall in love this easily. This was just a fling. Or rather, it would be if she could ever get Alex to cooperate, damn it!

JESSICA WAS HOME early. He heard her car pull into the driveway at a quarter to four. After glancing out the window to verify that it was her car, he crossed to the kitchen sink to wash the dust from his hands. When she still hadn't walked through the front door a few minutes later, he looked out the window again.

He found her sitting in her car, her arms draped on the steering wheel, her forehead propped on her arms. At first he thought she might be crying, but when she straightened, he saw a deep frown marring her forehead.

Finally she threw open the door to the Beemer and

stalked up the steps. Anger delineated every line of her body. Even through the glass, he could hear the tapping of her shoes on the pavement, followed by the sound of the key in the lock, the door clicking open. He waited for the resounding slam that was sure to follow. And waited.

He'd lived with women for most of his life. Every woman he'd ever known slammed doors when she was angry. But apparently Jessica, even well and truly pissed, did not.

After setting down the cordless screwdriver, he made his way to the living room, only to stop short when he found her leaning against the closed front door. Head tipped down, eyes closed, a frown entrenched on her face.

Dressed in a charcoal-gray dress and black jacket, black heels, her hair was pulled back into a twist, the way she always wore it. Her makeup pale and minimal. A single pearl dangled from the silver chain around her neck.

Like the pearl, Jessica was beauty without flash. Classiness almost to the point of delicacy. Lovely, but frail.

Then her eyes popped open.

No, not frail. Contained.

"You're home early."

"I wasn't getting any work done." She propelled herself away from the front door. Her skirt was tight enough to keep her steps small, but with each stride, her heels tapped crisply against the tile in the entry hall. She walked past him toward the bedroom, reaching to the back of her neck to open the clasp of her necklace.

"Wanna talk about it?"

She stilled, then spun on her heel, the necklace hanging from her fingertips. "Talk about what?"

"Whatever's got you so pissed off."

One perfectly sculpted blond eyebrow arched. Her chin

bumped up a notch and she managed to look down at him from across the room. "I don't know what you're talking about."

"Whatever." Angry women, he knew how to deal with. Chilly ones were something else entirely. So she made it three more steps down the hall before he added, "Your highness."

Her head snapped back around and she glared at him, her gaze no longer dismissive but openly confrontational. "What?"

That was better. If he diverted her anger toward him, he wouldn't worry about her snapping from the strain of keeping it under control.

"You were doing your princess impersonation. I just thought I'd play along."

She opened her mouth to shoot back a reply, but instead of skewering him, she sighed. "Sorry."

Propping his shoulder against the doorway between the kitchen and the living room, he asked again, "So, do you want to talk about it?"

She shook her head and he thought that would be the end of it. But instead of disappearing down the hall, she mimicked his stance, propping her shoulder against the doorway on the opposite side of the room.

"Tell me something, Alex, do you think of me as a good girl?"

"I'm not sure I know what you mean."

"I mean, do you think I'm a good girl?" She pushed away from the doorway and shrugged out of her jacket as she moved toward him. With each step, her hips swayed with the rhythm of her words. "A prissy, prim and proper good little girl."

He'd been right. Jessica was itching for a fight and there

was a seductive, sexual edge to her anger. Despite himself, he felt his body respond to her.

Since she was still waiting for an answer, he prevaricated. "I wouldn't say that."

"But you do think I'm a good girl, don't you?"

"What's your point, Jess?"

By now, she was standing directly in front of him, mere inches away.

"You think I'm a good girl. 'A princess,' you said. It's one of the things you find attractive."

"I—"

"I know you're attracted to me. I know you feel the same pull I do. Don't deny it, Alex." There was a pleading note in her voice. She all but begged him.

"I wasn't going to," he admitted.

Her eyes flashed with something like triumph. "So the only question, then, is, are you attracted to me just because you think I'm a good girl?"

Ah, so that's what this was about.

He had no idea what had brought this on, but he had to be honest with her.

"I do think you're a good girl, Jessica. But I also think you're more complicated than that. I think you're smart and funny. I think you're hardworking, and I admire that, because you've got enough money you don't have to be. I think—"

"The question is—" she cut him off, walking her fingers up his chest "—whether you're only attracted to the good girl in me. Because I'm tired of being good."

Her fingers traced distracting patterns on his chest, making it impossible for him to even think straight. She gazed up at him with those unbelievably blue eyes of hers and he felt something in him snap.

"I want to be naughty, Alex. I want to feel—what was it you called it?—pure gut-wrenching lust? That's what I want."

He struggled to get his body's response under control, but her fingers were driving him crazy. He backed away from her touch, trying to put some distance between them, but she followed him step for step until he felt himself bump into the kitchen counter behind him. He grabbed her hand in his to stop their progress across his chest.

"Jess, I don't know what brought this on, but with the mood you're in this would be a mistake. You'd—"

"I won't regret it. Promise. It's what I want. It's what we both want."

With her hand enclosed in his, she stepped closer to him, eliminating the space between them, trapping their joined hands between their bodies. She tugged their hands down so his knuckles brushed against her breast.

Her nipple puckered and hardened beneath his touch. Her eyelids drifted closed as her body arched into his.

"Come on, Alex, you've been a bad boy all your life. Stop trying so hard to be good."

12

SHE KNEW the instant his control snapped. One second, he'd been perfectly still, practically frozen. The next, she felt his hands everywhere. He grasped her around the waist and lifted her to the countertop.

His every touch sent shivers of pleasure through her body. The cool air against her skin, the heated touch of his rough and calloused fingertips. His were the hands of a worker. Strong. Used. Lived in.

She ached to feel them on other parts of her body. On her neck, her breasts. Between her legs.

She'd never wanted a man the way she wanted Alex. Never ached for a man this much. Never felt so incomplete without him.

She linked her calves behind his waist, pulling him even closer. Her dress bunched up almost to her crotch and the denim of his jeans scraped against the sensitive skin of her inner thighs. The sheer eroticism of having him between her legs had her gasping for breath. But knowing he wanted her as much was even more compelling.

He nuzzled her cheek, his mouth sliding slowly across her skin. When his lips finally met hers, his kiss was hotter and wetter than any she'd ever had before.

Heat and desire spiraled through her blood, pooling low in her gut and between her legs, making her ache with need. As if he knew exactly what she wanted, he grasped her hips and pulled her to him. She groaned as her tender flesh came into contact with him.

His penis was hard beneath the fabric of his jeans. Through the delicate silk of her panties she felt the ridge of his zipper and the heat of his erection.

Suddenly desperate to feel his skin against hers, her palms tingled as she tugged at the buttons of his plaid shirt.

The flesh she uncovered was hardened by years of manual labor, the muscles clearly defined. She couldn't help but marvel at the way they bunched and twisted beneath her hands.

His skin—so much darker than hers—was smooth except for a sprinkling of fine, coal-black hair across the vee of his chest.

No other man she'd ever been with had a chest like this, so dark and so hard. So used by life. Only Alex earned his living with these muscles, used them to destroy and to create. Only Alex.

The differences between their bodies fascinated her. His strength to her softness. The hard planes of his body to her curves. His dark tan to her pale skin. No one else so defined her by all that she wasn't. Only Alex.

Then she felt his hands on her back, at her zipper. He tugged it down in one smooth motion, baring her skin to his touch. She gasped as she felt his work-roughened fingers trace the length of her spine. Wanting to be closer to him, she struggled to free her arms from the dress.

When he tugged impatiently at her bra strap, she gently nudged his hands aside and undid the front clasp herself.

As she tossed her bra aside, she couldn't help but revel in his expression. His face was taut with desire as he looked at her bare breasts. For the first time in her life, she felt proud of her body, exhilarated by a man's reaction to it.

Once her arms were free, she braced her palms on the counter and lifted her hips as he pulled the dress down her legs and tossed it aside.

Sitting there, nearly naked on her kitchen counter, her breath coming in short bursts and her skin prickling against the cool air, she shivered, not from the cold but with anticipation, as he traced a single fingertip down her chest, then around her nipple. He brushed his thumb across the peak, his gaze focused intently on her response. She arched her back as her nipples hardened, all but begging for his touch.

"Please…" she heard herself gasp. Beg. "Please, Alex…"

His lips twitched. In an instant he went from so incredibly serious, to amused. "I like hearing you beg," he teased. "I could get used it."

So could I, she realized. Out loud, she said, "Please, Alex. Don't make me wait."

And he didn't. Ducking his head, he pulled her nipple into his mouth. She was nearly undone by the feeling of him suckling her breast, by the sight of his dark hair against her pale skin and his lush, sensual mouth on her breast.

Her legs clenched automatically around his hips, pulling him even closer. She bucked off the counter, rubbing her aching flesh against the length of his erection.

"Now, Alex," she gasped. "Please. Now."

He seemed not to respond, but continued lavishing attention on first one breast, then the other. His hands teasing her sensitive flesh, his teeth nipping at her skin, his breath warming her. Finally he looked up. Though his face was hardened with desire, his gaze hadn't lost that teasing glint.

"Tell me what you want," he ordered.

"You. I want you."

With one hand firmly on her back, the other traced a path down her belly, hovering just above her panties, which were moist with her desire for him. He slipped one fingertip beneath the elastic. "Be specific."

She nearly groaned. "You're enjoying this," she accused.

He had the gall to chuckle. "I'd rather hoped you were enjoying it, too."

Clutching at his shoulders, then his waist, she tried to urge him toward her. "You know what I want."

"Do I?" His finger withdrew to trace a path along her belly.

"Yes." She gasped as he rimmed the elastic at the leg hole of her panties before slipping his fingers inside to toy with the tender flesh. Arching against him, she moaned. "I want you."

"You want me to…"

"I want you inside of me. Please, Alex, make love to me."

She only had to ask once. With brusque movements, he fumbled for his wallet. She frowned, unsure what he was doing, frustrated that he'd stopped touching her, until she saw him pull a condom from the wallet before tossing it aside. As he tore the condom open, she reached for the closure to his jeans. She tore at the button and zipper, then pulled down his jeans and his boxers. Her hands trembled as she freed his erection. She had to concentrate to keep her movements gentle as she cradled him in her palm.

Almost reverently, she took the condom from him and eased it down his length. He seemed as affected as she felt as he pulled her panties down her legs and tossed them aside. Cradling her cheek with one hand and bracing the other on her hip, he kissed her long and deep before sliding her to the edge of the counter and thrusting up into her.

She shuddered as he filled her completely, pulling back from his kiss to gasp out his name. Clutching at his shoulders, her cheek pressed to his, she chanted, "Alex, please."

She gasped out the words with his every thrust. Tilting her hips forward, she accepted him more deeply inside her. It seemed he touched her very core, the heart of her. And with every thrust, he pushed deeper, driving her closer to the edge, until finally she dissolved around him as he thrust one last time, clutching her to him, gasping out her name.

JESSICA FELT SO GOOD in his arms, he hated to move. Still, he couldn't resist lowering his mouth to hers and kissing her one last time before leaving her bed. After making love to her in the kitchen, he'd carried her through the house to her bedroom where he'd loved her a second time. If he had his way, they'd never leave the bed again. Since that wasn't an option, he poured into the kiss all the emotions he couldn't share with her out loud.

When he finally pulled away from her, he had to clear his throat before speaking. "Didn't you say something about meeting your parents for dinner?"

For a second her expression remained soft and sensual. Then, as his words sank in and reality returned, she stiffened. "Damn."

Jumping to her feet, she swayed slightly before gaining her balance. Shaking her head as if to clear it, she stalked toward the bathroom. Stopping midstride, she swung around. "What time is it?"

He glanced at his watch, then rolled onto his side and propped himself up on his elbow to watch her. "A quarter to seven."

"Damn." She paused at the doorway. "I can be ready to go in ten minutes. Can you be ready to go by then?"

"You want me to go with you?"

"No! I—" She frowned. "I mean, will you be ready to leave when I leave. So I can lock up. But I guess you have my spare key, don't you?" Again she shook her head. Doubt etched the lines of her face where passion had been not so long ago. Doubt and something else, as well. "You don't…want to go. Do you?"

Whatever he might have said five minutes ago was irrelevant. He'd seen the absolute horror flicker across her face. She didn't want him to meet her parents. In fact, the very thought of him meeting her parents had drained the blood from her cheeks and shocked her system.

"No, I don't want to meet them."

"Good. I mean…they're not…it would be awkward, today since we just—" she waved her hand back and forth between them "—you know." Then, as if she'd just thought of it, she tacked on, "And they're not expecting you."

"I get it."

"You…" She hesitated. "You're not mad?"

"Not at all." The words stuck in his throat, but he forced them out.

She didn't even notice. She just sighed with relief and made her way to the bathroom.

He pulled on his clothes as he found them. Shoving his legs into his jeans, yanking on his shirt, ramming his feet into his work boots. Cursing himself every step of the way. What was wrong with him?

He didn't want to meet her parents. So why the hell was he so pissed off? Because it killed him that she didn't want him to meet them.

By the time she emerged from her bedroom, he was seated at the kitchen table, tying knots into his shoelaces.

"Have you seen my necklace? The pearl?"

She wore another one of her sleek, knee-length dresses, this one cream-colored with a long flowing scarf tied around her neck. Her hair was once again smoothed to the back of her head, her makeup once again flawless. The transformation from hot, sexy woman to icy princess was remarkable. And, just as she'd predicted, it had taken less than ten minutes. Hell, she ought to win some kind of an award for that.

"On the coffee table."

"Thanks."

By the time she fastened the necklace and picked up her purse, he was out the door and halfway down the walkway. When he heard her call out, he almost didn't stop.

"Alex, wait up."

But he did stop. Muttering a curse, he pivoted to face her. She turned the key in the lock then twisted the doorknob to verify she'd locked it before walking down the path to where he stood. Dusk had set in and the half light cast shadows across her face, highlighting the pure perfection of her bone structure as well as the frown that marred her forehead.

"When will I see you again?"

"I'll be back in the morning to finish knocking down the wall and to clean up the debris. After that, it'll be a couple of days before I make it back. The lumber and drywall won't be delivered until late next week."

"That's not what I meant. When will I see you?"

"What happened tonight was a mistake. We both know that."

She jerked back as if she'd been slapped. "A mistake? Alex, what are you talking about?"

He stepped closer and lowered his voice. "Come on, Jessica, you screwed around with the hired help. You've had your fling now. Don't tell me you thought this would develop into a long-term relationship."

"'The hired help'? Is that how you think I see you?"

He heard the surprise in her voice, but he was too pissed off to care. "It's pretty obvious how you see me." He took a step back, unable to stand being so close to her for much longer. "Look, it was fun, but I won't be waiting around for the novelty to wear off."

She grabbed his arm. "Alex, wait."

As tempted as he was to shake her off, he couldn't bring himself to do it. Not when she said his name like that. He looked down at her hand on his arm, then back up at her.

"I don't think that's fair. Not to either of us. What happened tonight was more than just a novelty." Doubt flickered across her face. "Wasn't it?"

Against his will, something inside him softened. "Do you really want to have this conversation right now? When you're already late for dinner with your parents?"

He'd been unable to keep the twinge of bitterness from his voice and her brows snapped together when she heard it.

"The dinner with my parents? Is that what this is all about?"

Now that it came down to it, he didn't want to say the words. And he sure as hell didn't want to hear her say them. But clearly she wasn't going to let this go. "Look, you

don't want me to meet them. That's fine. Can't say I blame
you."

"That's what you think? That I'm ashamed of you?" She
didn't give him a chance to answer, but closed the distance
between them and cupped his cheek in her palm. "It's not
you I'm ashamed of. It's them."

"Your parents?" Jeez, he'd never thought she'd lie about
it. "The senator and his wife? Right. They're the ones
you're ashamed of."

"You don't know what they're like—"

"Spare me the excuse." He jerked away from her touch.
"You're going to be late."

"No! Listen to me, damn it."

He stopped and leveled his gaze to study her. To really
look at her for the first time since she'd left the bed. Her
frown had deepened and her skin was even paler than nor-
mal. Her teeth worried at her lower lip.

"I'm serious, Alex. My parents can be…well, 'rude' is
the nicest way to say it. And they've always been particularly nasty to my boyfriends. And given your history with
my dad…"

He studied her face for signs she wasn't telling the truth
but found none. And despite himself, he couldn't help
being amused by the idea of Jessica trying to protect him.
He smiled wryly. "I can take care of myself."

She smiled in relief. "I'm sure you can. But you don't
know them. My father always grills men about how much
money they make and how their retirement funds are
doing. My mother's even worse. Just trust me. It's really
not you I'm worried about."

Her eyes begged him to believe her. He almost did. But
he watched her climb into her Beemer with a growing
sense of dread. His instincts told him she was being hon-

est, but he wasn't sure he could trust them. His instincts also told him to toss her over his shoulder, carry her back into her bedroom, lock the door and spend the next week making love to her.

And regardless of what his instincts said, a lifetime in this town told him sleeping with Jessica—no matter how pleasurable the experience might be—wouldn't solve anything.

She'd had her little fling with the town bad boy. She'd proven to herself that she wasn't boring, passionless or too good. For her, this had been nothing more than a means of self-expression. For him, it had been everything.

13

"DEAR, don't pick at your food."

Criticism number twenty-three. Not bad for less than thirty minutes. Among other things, they'd discussed, in nauseating detail, Jessica's clothing—too wrinkled, her hairstyle—too harsh, her job—too menial and her lipstick—entirely too bright.

She didn't bother to tell her mother that she wasn't wearing any. Any color in her lips had been put there the old-fashioned way. It'd been kissed into them.

Looking around the country club's main dining room, she couldn't help but see it in a different light. This room made up most of the wing that had been added in the late-eighties. Alex's uncle had worked on this room. Chances were good Alex had, as well.

For the first time she studied the dark oak paneling. The country club had originally been built back in the fifties. During the renovation it had been redesigned to look as if it had been built at the turn of the century, to match the architecture of downtown Palo Verde. The transformation had been miraculous. And Alex had been a part of it. In some small way, he'd been a part of building something that would last.

Had she ever, in the entire course of her career at Handheld Technologies, created something as wonderful?

"If you're not going to eat—" her mother's voice interrupted her thoughts "—just set your fork aside and be done with it. The way you're playing with it, you look like you've been afflicted by melancholia."

"Thank you, Mother, for your concern."

Her mother stiffened. "Jessica, is this really necessary?"

"What?"

"These occasional bouts of adolescent rebellion?"

"I don't know what you mean."

Her father cleared his throat, then shot a stern look in first her mother's direction and then in hers. Then he purposefully changed the subject. "So, Jessica, when are we going to see that boyfriend of yours again?"

She stilled instantly. "Boyfriend?"

"Yes, yes. Weren't you seeing someone from work before you went to Sweden?" Her father sliced off a bite of steak and popped it into his mouth.

"I went on a couple of dates, but it petered out long before I even left the country."

Her mother set down her fork with a beleaguered sigh. "I wish you'd told me. I've already bought tickets to the fund-raiser. I doubt I'll be able to return his."

"I did tell you." She had trouble keeping her frustration from her voice. "And the fund-raiser is for a good cause. I doubt an extra thousand dollars for cancer research will kill you."

Her mother at least had the good grace to look offended. "Well, of course not, but—"

"The campaign is going well." Jessica's father cut her mother off before she could continue. Not to avoid the argument, necessarily, but to turn the conversation back to him.

"That's nice, Daddy." Jessica sighed, wishing she

could return her attention to picking at her food. Frankly, she didn't care how the campaign was going, but not responding would create more trouble than simply listening.

Ever since he'd been elected to the senate, their conversations always felt as though she was being prepped for an interview. Midway through his dissertation on educational budget cuts, she interrupted him.

"What's your position on the new senate bill to help migrant farm workers?"

Her mother sighed. "Honestly, Jessica. Didn't you read any of the information I've given you about your father's platform?"

Refusing to be cowed, she met her mother's gaze head-on. "Actually, no I didn't."

Her mother bristled. "How many times—"

Her father placed his well-manicured hand over hers. "Now, Caroline..." He let his voice trail off, sending some silent, subtle message.

Her mother sipped her wine, but said nothing more.

"Well, Jessica, I'm glad you asked. As I'm sure you know, this is a complicated issue. Concerns for migrant farm workers must be balanced with the economic prosperity of the small family farm. Research shows that—"

She interrupted him again. "You have the opportunity to do wonderful things. How can you ignore that?"

Her mother slammed down her wineglass. "Is it really necessary to question your father's politics in public?"

Without giving her a chance to respond, her mother segued to another topic with an ease that left Jessica shaking her head. She wasn't allowed to discuss politics in public, but when was the last time she'd seen her parents in private? Months? Years?

At times like these, she felt as if she was only invited to these weekly dinners because it would look bad if conservative family man, Senator John Sumners, didn't see his daughter once a week.

But in her heart, she'd always felt that way. More a prop for her parents' political ambitions than a child. She knew now that they loved her in their own way…it was just a very distant, reserved way. But as a child, she'd yearned for her parents' affection. Except for all the times she'd been carted out for important social functions, she had few memories of her mother. The occasional whiff of Chanel No. 5 and vodka.

Jessica had fonder memories of their first housekeeper and cook, Mrs. Rivera, a comfortably round woman who dispersed giant hugs and homemade cookies with equal glee. Who smelled of homey vanilla mixed with the faint scent of exotic spices like cumin and coriander. Spices that never made it into the shrimp scampi or chicken cordon blue that graced the Sumners' dinner table.

Then one summer Jessica had been sent off to tennis camp, where she'd made no friends, learned almost nothing and repeatedly bonked her doubles partner with stray serves. She'd returned home to find Mrs. Rivera replaced by Mrs. Nguyen, a rail-thin Vietnamese woman whose French cooking was impeccable, but who smelled faintly of vapor rub and who never baked cookies.

For the first time in years, she thought of Mrs. Rivera, wondered what had happened to the woman once she'd left the Sumners household, and longed for a vanilla-scented hug. Almost immediately, she felt awash with shame. Why hadn't she thought of Mrs. Rivera in so many years? Why hadn't she cared enough to wonder what had become of the woman until now?

She hadn't lied to Alex earlier when she'd told him she was embarrassed by her parents. But she hadn't been entirely truthful, either. She was also embarrassed by herself.

She was at her worst when she was with them. In her deepest heart, she feared she could be just as pushy and self-centered and manipulative as they could be. It was something she didn't like to admit to herself. It was certainly something she didn't want Alex to know.

14

JESSICA STOOD on Alex's doorstep for a full three minutes before ringing the doorbell. It took her that long to muster up the fake, cheerful smile. If she'd waited to muster her courage, as well, she would have stood there until dark.

In the end, her fear of being discovered lurking on his porch outweighed her nerves. She hadn't seen him since they'd had sex, then fought about her parents immediately afterward. Not the best way to start a relationship—even a fling.

Showing up uninvited to a party wasn't the best start to a relationship, either, but here she was. When she'd left the house this afternoon, determined to smooth things over, she'd never anticipated stumbling into a full-blown bash.

Cars filled the driveway and overflowed to the curb to stretch the length of Alex's property and well beyond. Latin music, with a heavy beat and a seductive rhythm, drifted out through the open windows. Not at all what Alex usually listened to while he worked—which was jazz, surprisingly enough.

Finally the door swung open to reveal a middle-aged woman with graying hair and dark smiling eyes.

The woman asked a question in Spanish that Jessica had no hope of understanding.

Jessica choked out a surprised, "Hello," then frantically began sifting through her memory for any other scraps of sixth-grade Spanish.

The woman nodded, as if she understood Jessica's hesitation. "You are here to see Alejandro?" The woman asked in heavily accented English.

Ale-who? Jessica wondered for a second before her brain kicked in and she remembered Alex was the Anglicized form of Alejandro.

"Yes." Thank God, she hadn't been forced to respond with her limited Spanish vocabulary.

"Come in, come in."

As Alex's mother—who else could she have been?—led Jessica through the living room to the kitchen, she couldn't help thinking of her own mother, who received guests in the formal living room and who preferred to serve white wine and roasted Brie while strains of Chopin played softly in the background.

Today, the tiny kitchen was overflowing with women, most of whom had a child or two in tow. The scent of roasting meat and fresh tamales filled the air.

Alex's mom introduced her as merely a friend of Alex's and within minutes she'd met both of Alex's sisters and a bevy of cousins and children whose names she would never remember. Marisol—the oldest of his sisters—was petite and curvy, with sleek, cropped hair and sad, soulful eyes. Isabel—the younger sister—was nearly as tall as Alex with long, golden hair.

Within minutes of ringing the doorbell, Jessica had a drink thrust into her hand and was seated at the table with a child on her lap, like an old family friend. No one seemed to question why she was here, as if she'd been invited to whatever family gathering she'd stumbled into.

To make matters worse, she knew when Alex realized she'd arrived, he would not be happy. After all, if he'd wanted her here, he would have invited her himself.

As if her trepidation had conjured him, Alex appeared in the doorway an instant later. Through the open back door, she caught a glimpse of the backyard, men sitting around the picnic table, a couple of boys wrestling in the grass. A setting so cheerful and inviting she hated that she'd interrupted his day with his family.

If the expression on his face was any indication, he hated it even more.

She handed the child off to its mother and stood. "Hi. Sorry to bother you at home." Even as she apologized, she hated having to do it.

"No problem." He crossed the small kitchen and extracted her from the huddle of women before leading her into the living room. The moving boxes she'd seen on her first visit were gone and the furniture had been arranged around the fireplace on the far wall.

"It seems like you're having a party."

He nodded, and though he seemed reluctant to bring her into the loop, he explained, "My niece Miranda's ninth birthday."

Right. A family affair. Not the sort of thing to which one invites one's sexual partners. Well, she probably had that coming. She hadn't wanted him at the dinner with her parents. Why should he want her here?

"I just stopped by for a minute. I've got some news."

"Is it something about the house?"

"Sort of." She sat on the sofa, very aware of the voices in the kitchen, the buzz of curious women. Still, if he could be reserved and professional for the sake of his family, so could she. "Actually it's about your bid for the courthouse job."

He sat opposite her, legs stretched out in front of him. A flicker of annoyance crossed his face before he asked, "What about it?"

She reached into her bag and pulled out the pair of tickets her mother had given her. "The Annual American Cancer Society Gala at the country club."

She held her breath, waiting for his response. Which was not quite what she'd hoped for. Finally she said, "The annual gala is the one event no one misses."

"So?"

"So…the entire city counsel will be there. So will the county manager. More importantly, so will all the members of the historical society."

He continued to stare blankly at her.

"So…if you go to the gala you'll have the chance to schmooze with all the people who'll decide who gets the job."

Interest sparked in his gaze, but he quickly banked it. "You know I don't have a chance of getting that job."

"Why not? Someone has to get it, why not you?"

"Because this damn town—"

"Is not the same town it was fifteen years ago. But you have to give people the opportunity to see that you've changed, too."

He studied her face a moment before asking, "You really think going to this gala will do that?"

"Yes, I do. The city council and county manager are business people. They'll make their decision based purely on whether or not your bid is better than the others. But the historical society is something else entirely. If you come to the gala, it's going to impress them. If we're there together—"

"That'll just make it worse."

"Only if people think I'm ashamed to be seen with you. If we go to the party together, people will see you're not just the hired help I'm doing on the side. You're a businessman I happen to be dating." He still looked unconvinced, so she threw in, "Even if you don't get the courthouse job, you'll still meet people, potential clients. Come on, Alex. It can't hurt."

"I'll think about it," he finally agreed.

"Think about what?"

Jessica turned to see Alex's mother standing in the doorway, drying her hands on a dishtowel. Sensing a potential ally, Jessica stood and held out the tickets. "I'm trying to convince Alex to attend the American Cancer Society gala with me. He doesn't want to, but it would be very good for his business."

His mother raised her eyebrows, looking very much the way Alex did when he was skeptical. "What is this…" She hesitated, as if trying to wrap her tongue around an unfamiliar word. "…gala?"

"It's a big party. A lot of potential clients and influential people will be there."

Alex's mother frowned and the confusion in her eyes highlighted Jessica's mistake.

Anxiety knotted her stomach. She simply didn't know what words to use. "I mean—"

Before she could fumble any more, Alex finished the sentence for her in Spanish.

"Ah!" His mother nodded in understanding, then smiled at Jessica. "Sometimes my English is—" she held out her hand, palm down, twisting it in a so-so gesture "—not so good."

"Oh, no, Mrs. Moreno," she protested automatically. "It's excellent."

Alex's mother beamed. "Please, call me Rosa." Linking arms with Jessica, she led her back toward the kitchen. "My boy tells me *nada*. He doesn't want me to worry, he says. How can I not worry?"

Mrs. Moreno—no, Rosa—didn't give her a chance to reply. "You'll stay for dinner, *sí*?" In a voice filled with awe she explained, "Alejandro paid for José and I to fly up to Sacramento for Miranda's birthday. José and the boys are making *carnitas*. The girls and I are making tamales. You can help."

The decision was made before Jessica could even think of an excuse. In the kitchen, Rosa poured Jessica another drink and put her to work rolling tamales.

The other women smiled broadly when Rosa explained about the gala, but Jessica could see the questions in their eyes. They were all wondering who she was and what claim she had on their brother.

And Alex wasn't talking. However, his feelings about the subject were quite obvious. A scowl settled onto his face as he stood with his arms crossed over his chest and his shoulder propped against the door to the kitchen. Even after his mother shooed him out to the backyard with the rest of the men, Jessica could still feel his irritation looming over her.

Telling his mother about the gala may have bought her more time in which to convince him, but it had pissed him off. And sooner or later she'd have to deal with him. Frankly, she was hoping it'd be later.

HAVING JESSICA meet his family—his entire big, loud, pushy family—all at once was the last thing he'd wanted. That's why he hadn't told her his parents had come up for the weekend.

His family was bad enough in small doses. Not that he didn't love them…he did. But he was also painfully aware of how different they were from Jessica's family. Not that he'd met her parents, but he could imagine. In fact, he'd caught a glimpse of the senator and his wife on the local news the other night. At a thousand-dollar-a-plate political fund-raiser.

Shit. A thousand dollars a plate. He could feed his entire extended family for a fraction of that. While he'd watched that news clip he couldn't help imagining how that smiling, slick couple would react if they knew he was sleeping with their daughter. Him, the son of a dirt-poor migrant farm worker, a guy who made his living with his hands. A guy who couldn't even begin to pay a thousand dollars a plate to eat dinner with Senator Sumners.

He couldn't help thinking about the damn political dinner and wondering how many of those things Jessica had attended over the years. And how this cheap backyard barbecue couldn't even compare.

He spent the whole day waiting for her to make her excuses and leave. Surprisingly, she didn't.

She'd worn the sexy little skirt and sweater she'd bought the day they'd gone shopping together. The skirt accented her slim hips and long, shapely legs. Bright pink toenail polish peeked through the open toes of her sandals. As always, her hair was slicked back and knotted low at the back of her head, exposing the elegant length of her neck and the slender silver chain from which her pearl dangled.

He'd watched as she'd helped roll tamales. With each tamale, she'd scrunched up her eyes and bit her lip in concentration.

By the time his mother called them all for lunch, he'd been more than ready for her to leave.

He watched in dread as his mother led Jessica to the table and seated her between Isabel and Luis, who was back from college for the weekend.

"Don't look so worried," Tomas murmured as he slid into the chair next to him.

"I'm not worried."

Tomas laughed. "Yeah, right. Look, she's doing fine." Tomas reached across him for the salad bowl. "You, on the other hand, look ready to have a seizure. Calm down."

"That's easy for you to say. That wasn't your girlfriend out there drinking Uncle Sal's home-brewed beer."

Tomas clapped him on the back. "Don't worry. Uncle Sal's home brew has never killed anyone. Yet." As they'd watched, Jessica had taken a tentative sip of the beer. She'd blanched only for a second before pasting on a bright smile. "It takes a while to get used to. And she's probably not normally a beer drinker."

"Right. That's it."

"What? You think she's not enjoying herself?"

"Look around, Tomas," Alex mocked. "She's the daughter of a senator. They have their family parties at the country club. She's got a trust fund, for Christ's sake. Do you think this is her kind of party?"

"Hey, she's getting along great. You're the one who's uncomfortable."

And she did seem to be getting along great. As he watched, eighteen-month-old Beatrice, the youngest of Isabel's three children, toddled over to Jessica and held up her arms.

This would be it. The thing that pushed her over the edge and sent her running for the door.

He sat back, ready to go to her rescue. But before he could even stand, she set down her fork and reached for the child. She picked up Beatrice awkwardly, her inexperience clear in her stiff movements and worried expression. Beatrice didn't seem to notice. She curled up against Jessica's chest, grabbed a lock of blond hair with one hand and reached for a tortilla with the other.

Beatrice gummed the tortilla, drooling occasionally, but otherwise sat peacefully in Jessica's lap while Jessica made conversation with Isabel.

Beatrice didn't even look out of place in Jessica's arms, and Jessica even seemed to relax further, the longer the toddler was in her lap.

She fed Beatrice bites of *masa* and chunks of the pulled pork his father had roasted overnight. When Beatrice waved a greasy fist near Jessica's sweater, Jessica captured the girl's hand in her own. Alex waited, fully expecting her to hand Beatrice back to Isabel. Instead, Jessica brought Beatrice's tiny hand to her lips and nipped playfully at her fingers. Giggles erupted from Beatrice, mingling with Jessica's melodic laughter.

Watching her, he felt his heart fill with something that felt terrifyingly close to love. Not just the adolescent, lust-driven puppy love he'd been battling for so long, but something far more complicated. He was glad she'd come, yes, and he was glad she was getting along with his family. But it was more than that. He wanted her here. Not just today, but always. He wanted to stand here, to watch her feed bites of *masa* to *their* child.

He knew in that instant how completely he'd been fooling himself about his feelings for Jessica. This wasn't just lust. This wasn't even just infatuation. This was the real deal.

And that scared the hell out of him.

Beside him, Tomas took a long swig of beer. When he set down the bottle he said, "See? She's doing fine."

"For now," Alex admitted. Though she was doing far better than he ever would have imagined.

But maybe he should have expected this. After all, her father was a politician. She was probably very skilled at this kind of thing. She'd even had a term for it. What had she called it? Conversational sleight of hand.

No wonder she seemed to fit so easily into the family.

"Tell me something, Alex. What's got you more worried? The fear that she wouldn't get along with the family or the fear that she would?"

He shot Tomas an irritated look. "Don't you have anything better to do than annoy me?"

The sound of Tomas's laughter grated his already raw nerves. "As a matter of fact, I do. I promised the kids a game of basketball after lunch."

With that, Tomas collected his now-empty plate and rose from his chair. Alex didn't bother to offer to join in the game. He couldn't take his eyes off Jessica. And he didn't want to.

With Tomas's words echoing in his ears, he consider for the first time that he might have been wrong about Jessica. All this time, he'd assumed their relationship had no future outside the bedroom.

Yet she'd spent most of the day with his family. And she seemed to be enjoying their company.

Were these really the actions of a woman who wanted a quick, passionate fling and nothing more?

They didn't seem to be.

Until now, he'd assumed Jessica would never settle for a relationship with someone like him, someone from a poor family who worked with his hands for a living. But what was it she'd said earlier? That people would only look down on their relationship if they thought she was ashamed to be with him. Those words implied she *wasn't* ashamed to be with him. Was it possible that all his fears about not being good enough for her were all in his head?

Everything he knew about her indicated she wasn't interested in a long-term relationship. But what if everything he knew about her was wrong?

"—BUT, YOU KNOW ALEX. He would never let us fight our own battles. He was up at the dean's office giving them hell until things got sorted out."

Luis and Isabel both laughed at the story. Jessica played along, though laughing was the last thing she felt like doing. Alex's brother and sister had been regaling her with stories about him for the past hour. With every "You know Alex" they tossed out, she felt less and less that she did.

The worst was when they'd forget she was there and slip into Spanish. When they referred to him as Alejandro, she felt as if they were talking about someone she'd never even met.

Oh, they'd catch themselves, apologize and repeat what they'd said in English. But every time it happened was a reminder that she just didn't belong here.

As the afternoon had drawn on, more and more people had shown up. Cousins and friends mingled by the picnic tables. All part of a vibrant and complex community she hadn't even known existed in Palo Verde. Alex had stood under the trees talking to the uncle he'd worked for as a teenager. The yard was decorated with casual spontaneity, streamers thrown up into the branches of the apple trees, white Christmas lights draped from limb to limb. The card table set up by the back door sagged under the weight of the desserts and treats. The party was barely planned, but lovingly executed in a way none of her own childhood birthday parties had ever been. Hers had been implemented with all the detail and emotional warmth of military action in the Gulf.

She took another sip of the margarita someone had poured her and looked longingly toward the door. Would it be wrong to leave before the birthday girl finished opening her presents? Would it matter, since she didn't even have a present for Miranda?

And that was the problem with crashing a party. You never knew what to bring.

Before she could make her escape, Miranda interrupted them. "Daddy said to tell you it's time for cake," the girl said solemnly.

Isabel rushed away to find paper plates and plastic forks. Luis followed to help carry the cake. Which left Jessica alone with the little girl.

Miranda, a tiny, darker-haired version of her mother, was already striking. She had black hair, which fell in baby-fine ringlets around her shoulders. Her eyes were large, like those of a Disney cartoon heroine. And—faced with a stranger—she bit nervously on her lower lip. Her gangly arms clutched a fat hardcover book close to her chest.

Finally the girl thrust out the book for Jessica to see. "It was a gift from Tío Alejandro."

Jessica accepted the book and studied its cover for a moment before asking, "Do you like Harry Potter?" The girl nodded. "Then I'm sure you'll enjoy having your mother read the book to you."

Miranda stiffened. "I'll read it myself." She must have sensed Jessica's disbelief, because, as she snatched the book back, she explained, "I've already read all the others."

"I'm impressed," Jessica admitted, though she had no idea what books other nine-year-old girls read.

"I read very well for my age," Miranda stated proudly. "Tío Alejandro said my book was from you, too. But I think he was just being nice because you forgot my present."

Jessica winced. "Well, you know Alex."

Miranda stared blankly at her.

Suddenly inspired, Jessica reached for the clasp of her necklace. "Actually, I did bring you a gift. I just didn't wrap it." She held out the silver chain to Miranda.

For a long moment Miranda merely stared at her. Finally she shifted the book to one hand and with the other, reached out to touch the pearl with the tip of her finger. "It's pretty." Her wide gaze met Jessica's. "Is it really for me?"

She hesitated only a moment. "Of course. Turn around and I'll put it on."

Miranda carefully set her book down on the chair, then turned her back to Jessica and held her hair out of the way.

As she fastened the necklace around Miranda's delicate neck, Jessica felt an odd tug deep inside. Very similar to the tug of emotion she'd felt holding Beatrice earlier. Alex's family was getting to her. Much as the man himself had.

When she looked up, she found Alex watching her once again. Throughout the day, it seemed every time her gaze sought him, he was already looking at her. The look in his eyes—one of dark intensity—made her shiver.

For an instant she almost forgot that he hadn't wanted her here. That he hadn't wanted her to meet his parents and his family. For an instant, she was lost in the intimacy of his gaze. Then the moment passed and she shook herself back to the present.

Miranda had skipped over to her grandfather and was pulling him toward Jessica. Alex's father was shorter than any of his children by several inches. What he lacked in height, he made up for in presence. With his lean, muscled body and impeccable posture, he seemed a much bigger man than he was. Though she could see why Alex worried about him. He moved like a man who'd lived hard years, slowly and with caution. His sun-darkened skin a badge of the seasons he'd spent working in the apple orchards of the northern valley and the citrus orchards of Arizona.

"*Abuelo,*" Miranda said. "Look at the necklace Miss Jessica gave me."

Though he moved slowly when he knelt beside his granddaughter, his eyes sparkled as he spoke to her in a flurry of Spanish that Jessica had no hope of understanding.

Miranda blushed and shook her head. Then, clutching her book in one hand and the pearl pendant between the fingers of her other, she turned back to Jessica. "Thank you, Miss Jessica."

"You're welcome, Miranda."

"Go get your cake," José said, then patted her on the behind as she scurried away to her mother. He watched her, smiling, until she was by her mother's side, then made his way to the chair beside Jessica.

As he lowered himself to the chair, her mind raced. She spoke almost no Spanish and he spoke very little English. Besides, she just didn't know what to say to him.

Lately she'd spent some free time at the office doing research online about migrant farm workers. But asking him how he felt about the use of pesticides in modern agriculture seemed inappropriate.

So instead, she said nothing.

He smiled broadly at her and she found herself smiling

back, hoping that could communicate how thankful she was to have been included today, how special his family had made her feel.

Finally, in halting English, he began to speak to her. "My boy, Alejandro…he is a good boy."

Her gaze automatically sought Alex in the crowd. At some point, the music had been turned up. Luis had pulled Marisol out into the yard and, along with several other couples, they danced beneath the lantern-strewn branches of the apple trees. Alex was out there dancing, as well. Holding Beatrice close to his chest, he danced her around the yard. The sight was so sexy, so heart-stoppingly masculine, her breath caught in her throat.

A good boy? Oh, he was so much more than that.

To his father, she merely said, "Yes, he is."

He nodded, seemingly satisfied with her limited answer. "I want Alex to…" He struggled for the right word, then settled on, "To do good."

She nodded her understanding.

Then he turned his gaze to her. "You will help."

"Yes," she said. "I will help." She was trying to anyway. If only he'd let her.

When she glanced back at Alex's father, she found him smiling slyly at her. Then he stood and extended his hand to her to help her up. Instead of releasing her hand when she stood, he draped it over his arm and led her to where the others were dancing to the heavy Latin beat. Their exuberant movements were a far cry from the sedate, mandatory dancing she'd done at the country club.

"Come. We'll dance."

When she pulled back, he stopped, looking at her with a raised eyebrow and questioning eyes, much the way Alex did so often.

"I don't know how," she explained. Not really a lie. She'd never before danced with such joy.

"*¿Por qué no?*"

"I don't know how." At his blank stare, she took an exaggerated, lumbering step and made to crunch his toes.

He laughed, nodding his understanding. Then shrugged as if to say "So, what?" He tugged again on her hand, but she refused to move.

With a sigh, he repeated her gesture, then tapped his fingers on her chest, just above her heart. "Here?" Then he tapped his fingers on her temple. "Or here?"

This time when he pulled on her hand, she allowed herself to be led out on the impromptu dance floor. Though the song was an upbeat Tejano tune, he held her as if they were waltzing. His feet moved smoothly in time to the music and, with his hand firmly on her back, she found it easy to let him lead.

But she didn't dance with Alex's father for long. Soon she was passed off to Tomas, who made her laugh so hard she really did step on his toes. Finally, he begged off and handed her to Alex.

Her breath caught when she felt herself wrapped in Alex's strong arms. They hadn't been alone all day. Though they were hardly alone now, the flickering lights from the tree branches created an intimacy that seemed to shelter them from the rest of the crowd.

His hand felt warm and strong against her back. It seemed the most natural thing in the world when he slipped his hand under the hem of her sweater to rest on her bare skin.

He cradled her hand closer to their bodies and she instinctively leaned in close to him. He smelled of sunshine and the roasted cumin from the *carnitas.*

"I saw you give your necklace to Miranda," he murmured, his words brushing against her ear. "You didn't have to do that."

She pulled back just enough to meet his gaze. "I didn't have anything else to give."

In the half light, his eyes looked pure black, his expression unreadable. Finally he nodded.

"I'll make sure Isabel knows its worth. Miranda will only wear it on special occasions."

She almost told him not to bother. Wasn't it more important the girl enjoy the necklace?

But that was the attitude of a rich girl…someone accustomed to buying and having expensive things. For the first time she considered that Alex's family might think such an expensive gift inappropriate from someone practically a stranger. So she said nothing.

One song passed into the next and then the next. Finally, when the burden of silence was too heavy, she spoke. "Alex, today's been nice. Your family is…" She let her words trail off, having no way to express how kind and welcoming they'd been.

"Crazy? Loud? Overwhelming?"

She laughed. "No. Well, yes. But wonderful."

As inadequate as that was, she didn't know what else to say. His mother, who treated her with such generosity. His brothers and sisters, who made her laugh and had been so kind. And his father, who with a few words of broken English had displayed more emotion than her father ever had, with the entire English language at his disposal.

To him, his family may be crazy, loud and overwhelming.

But to her? To her, they were a bit of Alex she never would have seen otherwise.

And her heart ached to think this was a part of him she'd never see again.

"WHERE'D YOU disappear to?"

Jessica started guiltily at the sound of Alex's voice. Slowly she turned to face him. Only the moonlight overhead and the faint light shining through an uncurtained window illuminated his form. He stood several feet behind her, midway down the driveway that ran alongside his house. His hands were propped on his hips.

She gestured toward her car, which was parked at the curb. "I thought I'd head out."

"You weren't going to say goodbye?"

"You were busy with your parents." She shrugged. The party in the backyard was still very much in full swing. She didn't want to demand his attention. Moreover, she didn't want to explain how lonely she'd suddenly felt among his family.

For a brief time, she'd felt a part of them. Though she knew that was only an illusion brought on by their friendliness, she couldn't help yearning to be a part of it for real.

"Thank your mom for making me feel so welcome," she said, slowly edging her way toward her car.

Alex followed her, the gravel of the driveway crunching under his feet with every step. "Stay and tell her yourself."

"No. I've stayed too long as it is. I've intruded enough."

"Don't go."

"Why would you want me to stay? You didn't want me here in the first place."

He ducked his head, a lock of hair falling across his forehead. "I never said that."

But he didn't deny it, either. "You didn't have to. You didn't invite me to meet your family."

Finally he caught her hand and held it, tugging it gently to pull her closer to him. At either end of the driveway, climbing roses grew up the sides of the house, shielding them from the backyard as well as from the street. "It's not that I didn't want you here. They can be…"

"Overwhelming? You said that earlier. I thought they were wonderful," she admitted. "I felt like part of the family."

He laughed ruefully. "The bad news is, now you practically are. Now that Mom knows we're dating, she'll inundate you. She'll call you. Bring you food." He interlaced his fingers with hers. "That's why I didn't invite you today. I didn't want them to scare you off."

She straightened her shoulders. "I don't scare easily."

But that wasn't necessarily true. The longing she felt when he talked about her being a part of his family terrified her. Despite what he said, spending a single afternoon with them didn't make her belong. Only Alex could do that, and she knew how unlikely that was.

Shoving that thought from her mind, she asked, "Have you decided about the gala?"

He stiffened and she sensed his withdrawal from her. "No."

"You really should come. It's the kind of thing that will make or break you."

"So you keep reminding me," he said, his tone harsh.

Sensing he was even more annoyed than he was letting on, she tried to explain. "I just meant that—"

"I know what you meant."

Yet, somehow she didn't think he did. She reached out to put her hand on his arm. Feeling his muscles tense beneath her touch, she added, "Alex, your family is very proud of you. They want you to be successful."

His gaze may have flashed with irritation, but the lighting was too dim and his eyes too dark for her to know for sure. She wanted to press him for an answer about the gala or to find out what she'd done to annoy him, but before she could, he closed the gap between them, then slowly backed her up to the wall behind her. The open kitchen window was just a few feet above her head. Through it drifted the faint Spanish of his family's conversation, interrupted occasionally by the clinking of plates and banging of pans.

"This is the first time we've been alone all day," he murmured. "Do you really want to talk about the gala?"

"Alex, don't." But there was no force behind her words. "Your family…" She looked up toward the window above her.

"Is all busy doing other things." He edged closer to her, nudging his knee between her legs. With one hand, he brushed a loose strand of hair away from her face. The other he ran up and down her arm.

His calloused fingertips felt deliciously rough against her bare skin. "They'll see us." But her protests sounded weak even to her own ears. She pressed her palm to his chest, trying to wedge some distance between them, but there was no strength behind her hand.

"They won't," he insisted, nudging her knees further apart, pressing into her body. "The roses block their view." He leaned in closer, barely kissing the corner of her mouth. "No one will see us. No one will know we're here."

She glanced from side to side. He was right. They were almost completely hidden by the climbing vines. Surrounded by dark green leaves, tiny white flowers and the fragrance of roses mingling with the intoxicating scent of warm male skin.

Her pulse kicked into high gear. The illusion of their solitude was enough for her body. She widened her stance, making room for his thigh to press against the juncture of her legs.

Part of her knew this was a mistake. Someone could walk around the corner at any minute. But at the same time, she didn't care. All she cared about was the burning ache inside her. The need to feel his body pressed against hers. The reassurances of how much he wanted her—physically, if not emotionally.

She tilted her chin upward as he lowered his mouth. She acquiesced immediately, opening her lips to his. His mouth was hot and impatient, ruthlessly coaxing a response from her. Not that he had to work hard.

A few hot kisses, the feel of his hands on her bare skin, that was all it took. When she felt him slide his hands up her ribcage to her breasts, she was gone.

Her passion hit quickly, unexpectedly. She'd spent the day cut adrift. Near him, but not with him. And as risky as it was to be with him right now, she needed it. Needed the affirmation that he still wanted her. That even while their relationship was rife with so many questions, this at least she knew and understood: he wanted her. Needed her, just as she needed him.

She clutched at his shoulders, rotating her hips to rub herself against him. She could feel his erection through his jeans, but her skirt was in the way. Almost without realizing what she was doing, she reached down and pulled her skirt farther up her thighs, giving her room to widen her legs. She moaned when she felt the hard length of his thigh come in contact with her crotch.

"Ah, Jess," he murmured in her ear.

"Please, Alex," she gasped. "Please tell me you have a condom with you."

He froze. Then cursed. "I don't."

She squeezed her eyes closed, trying to hide her frustration. "Can you come by tonight?"

"Yes." Then he cursed again. "No. My parents are staying at the house."

She nearly groaned out loud.

"Shh," he murmured. "It's okay."

His hand slid up her thigh, pushing her skirt further out of his way. He gently moved her panties aside to stroke the aching folds of her flesh. She gasped at the touch of his fingers.

"Shh," he murmured again as his other hand crept over her mouth, cutting off her panting gasps. She felt one finger and then another slide inside her. His thumb found her clitoris. His touch was soft, but his fingers rough.

The gentle stroking of his thumb edged everything else from her consciousness. As if from very far away, she heard a car pass on the street. The voices from the kitchen and yard faded to nothing. Soon, all she could hear was the faint rhythm of the music, the ragged tempo of his breath against her ear and the thrumming of her own blood.

All she could feel was the heat of his hands, the strength of his body and the touch of his fingers, pushing her closer and closer to the edge. As if her entire body and soul were condensed down to that one tiny nub of flesh. Balanced on a precipice. Waiting for him to push her over. And then he did. Her muscles spasmed around his fingers, her heart pounded against his chest and his mouth captured her moans of pleasure.

15

WELL, SHE'D WANTED to be saucy. Surely fooling around with a guy within earshot of his entire family ranked pretty high on anyone's list of saucy behavior.

Fooling around? the conservative prude buried deep inside of her asked. *That's a bit of an understatement.*

Ignoring the voice, she tugged her skirt down, pulling it back into place. She ran one hand, then both, over her hair, smoothing it and twisting it into a knot before she realized her bobby pins were scattered all over the ground, lost forever.

Through all of her efficient straightening of her clothes, she searched frantically for something—anything—appropriate to say. But she was woefully inexperienced in such matters and completely at a loss.

Alex, however, seemed relatively unfazed. He nudged her chin up with his knuckle, forcing her to look him in the eye. "Jessica, why don't you come inside with me? Stay for the rest of the evening?"

After what they just did? No way. Under the circumstances, she was having enough trouble meeting his gaze. Meeting his parents' would be impossible.

"No. Thank you." She reached for her bag, which she'd dropped at some point. "I'd rather just go home."

She'd expected more of an argument. Instead he nodded. "Okay." And fell into step beside her as she walked down the driveway toward her car.

When she climbed into the driver's seat, he braced his forearm on the roof and leaned in through the open door. "Jess, I—" He broke off abruptly, shaking his head ruefully. "I'll see you tomorrow."

"About the gala—"

"Don't worry," he said with a tired sigh. "I'll be there."

Then he planted a quick kiss on her mouth before straightening and closing the door. With his hands fisted on his hips, he stood on the curb, watching as she shifted the car into gear and drove down the street toward town.

As she made her way home, she couldn't shake the feeling that they'd left so much unsaid. Despite their intense physical attraction, they had almost nothing in common. Today more than proved that.

The obvious closeness and open affection of his family only made her uncomfortable. And at the same time, it made her ache with jealousy. In some ways, it seemed they spoke another language...in addition to the fact that they actually spoke another language. Beyond that barrier, so many other things differentiated them.

The thought left a sick feeling of dread deep in the pit of her stomach. As she pulled into her driveway and stared up at her own house, she realized she'd never even had her family over for dinner. Not once in the five years she'd lived here.

But as soon as she resolved to change that, an image of her mother popped into her head. She imagined her mother's lips curling in distaste as she said, "Really, dear, it's so much more convenient to meet at the country club."

By convenient, her mother would mean, less messy, both physically and emotionally. No dishes to clean up, no personal conversations to steer clear of. No one discussed emotional issues at the country club, so eating there was a way of keeping all of that at bay. More convenient, indeed.

Was this really the world she wanted to introduce Alex to?

Now that she'd talked the gala up both to him and his parents, did she have a choice?

"LET ME SEE if I've got this right. In the three weeks Brad and I were gone, you've given up your career goals, demolished your kitchen and hopped into bed with Alex Moreno."

Mattie sat cross-legged in the center of Jessica's bed. Her brown hair was streaked with blond from her time spent in the sun. Her arms were tanned, her nose and shoulders pink. She'd never looked better. Funny, how being loved did that for a woman. Made her bloom.

Watching Mattie, Jessica felt a pang of longing well up inside of her, but she ruthlessly squashed it back down. With a sigh, she rose from her bed and headed for her closet. "I haven't abandoned my career goals. I've just stopped obsessing on them. But otherwise, that about sums it up."

Mattie shook her head, either in confusion or exasperation. "I was only gone three weeks."

"Hey, I was gone for nine weeks and you fell in love with my brother. By the time I got back, you'd planned the wedding."

"That's different." Mattie stiffened. "Brad and I have a history."

"Well, Alex and I have a history."

"You had a crush on him in high school. That's it."

"That's not entirely true."

Mattie frowned, suddenly suspicious. "What else was there?"

As simply as she could, she told Mattie what had happened that day at the creek and explained how she and Alex had ended up exchanging notes. When she was done, she studied Mattie but couldn't gauge her reaction.

Mattie shook her head with a sigh. "And you never told me?"

Wincing at the accusation in Mattie's voice, she said, "There didn't seem to be much to tell. They were just notes." But even as she said it, she recognized how much more to her they'd been.

"Were you in love with him?"

"I hardly knew him. But in those notes, he was… different than I would have thought. Smarter and more sensitive. I wished I could have known him better, but he stopped writing to me. I couldn't hold his interest even then."

"Jess—"

Hoping to end the conversation, Jessica headed for her closet. "Do you want to borrow a dress for the gala or not?"

Mattie followed her into the closet, but didn't even glance at any of the gowns. "Okay, so you guys exchanged some notes, but that's not a history. At least not the kind of history you base a relationship on."

A relationship? No. But a wild fling based on pure gut-wrenching lust?

"It's not a relationship."

"Then what is it?"

Mattie's voice was filled with concern. Concern that normally would have comforted Jessica, but today just grated on her nerves. "It's just sex, okay?"

"Jessica—"

"Look, I know what I'm doing. I don't have any illusions about where this is going. I know it's based on sex and nothing else and I'm okay with that. You should be, too."

Patricia rushed into the room, breathless. "I hope it's okay I let myself in. I got here as quickly as I could. Are we looking at dresses yet?"

"We're trying to," Jessica muttered. Hoping Mattie would take a hint.

She didn't.

"I'm just worried about you, that's all."

Patricia's ears perked up. "Worried? Why? Because she's dating that really hot guy?"

"Yes," Jessica said, rolling her eyes.

"No," Mattie said at the same time. "I'm worried because you're not dating him. You're just sleeping with him. And I'm not sure you're capable of having a sex-only, no-emotion kind of relationship."

"But—"

Mattie cut Jessica off before she could even finish the thought. "Oh, I know you think you can. I'm sure you've got it all planned out how you're going to sleep with him, but stay emotionally detached and how it'll all work out for the best."

Patricia waggled her eyebrows speculatively. "Sounds to me like someone is speaking from experience."

"Exactly! It's no different than my big plan to seduce Brad as a way of getting over him. And look what happened to me."

"You fell in love, got married and are happy," Patricia pointed out.

"Yes, that's what I'm saying." She looked pointedly at

Jessica and, when she got no response, she turned her gaze on Patricia. "Help me out here."

Patricia merely shook her head. "I don't see your point."

"Don't…" Mattie practically sputtered in frustration. She looked back at Jessica, who finally took pity on her.

"Don't worry. I see your point. But you're wrong. I'm not in love with Alex. I'm not going to fall in love with Alex. I'm not. I promise. This is just one more thing to cross off my list."

Mattie threw up her hands in exasperation. "Don't even get me started on that stupid list."

"Hey, now." Patricia narrowed a steely glare at Mattie. "Don't be dissing The List."

Mattie rolled her eyes. "Seriously, it's just about the silliest—"

Before either woman could launch into a full-scale attack, Jessica interrupted them. "Look, Mattie, it's okay if you think The List is silly. But I don't." She grasped Mattie's hand, desperate to make her understand. "It's made me rethink my life. In a good way. It's made me try things I never would have done otherwise and that's exciting for me."

Mattie's frown deepened, then she sighed. "If you really feel like you need The List, fine. But it's not like you're doing *everything* on that list anyway. It's not like you're going to 'Go Tribal' and get something pierced."

"Actually…"

Mattie went white. "Dear God, don't tell me you got a tattoo!"

"No! You know I can't stand pain."

Patricia all but beamed. "Which is why I made her an appointment tomorrow to have Mendhi body painting done."

"Mendhi?" Mattie asked skeptically.

"It's temporary," Jessica hastened to reassure her.

"It's traditional Indian body painting done with henna to celebrate transcendence and transformation. As in, our little Jessica transcending her previous, boring existence and transforming into a *Saucy* woman." For a second Patricia sounded very serious and downright serene. Then she winked salaciously and added, "Besides, it's very sexy."

"So that's the last of The List, then?" Mattie asked.

"Just about."

In truth, there were several items left on The List—Drop the Drawers and Live in the Fast Lane she had plans for. Within the next forty-eight hours, she'd have done everything on The List, with the exception of number ten—Conquer It. Overcoming her worst fear.

The problem was, right now, her worst fear was that Mattie's words of caution had come too late. She was terrified that she already loved Alex.

As if she could sense Jessica's thoughts, Mattie's frown deepened. "Are you sure you know what you're doing?"

"I'm positive."

"Because—"

"I'm positive," she repeated firmly. But Mattie looked utterly unconvinced.

Actually, she looked about as unconvinced as Jessica felt.

As she, Mattie and Lucy dug through the dozen or so formal dresses she'd worn to country club events over the years to find one for Mattie to borrow, she kept trying to convince herself.

She did a decent job of faking carefree cheerfulness for their sake, burying her dread deep down inside. As her eyes drifted time and again to the red satin, vintage gown she'd picked out to wear to the gala herself, she chanted the words like a mantra. I'm not in love with Alex Moreno.

I'm not in love with Alex Moreno.

I'm not in love with Alex Moreno.

Once again, she found herself wishing for a pair of ruby-red slippers,

She eyed the high-heeled satin shoes she'd had dyed to match the dress. If she clicked her heels three times while chanting her new mantra, would that make it any more true?

16

HE'D NEVER WORN a tux before and frankly it was damn uncomfortable. But there were some things worth the discomfort of a starched shirt and rented shoes. The sight of Jessica poured into red satin was one of them.

From the front, the dress was relatively modest, cut well above her breasts, with thick straps that looped from her shoulders down to her waist. However, when she turned her back to him to lock her front door, the back of her dress was…missing. Soft folds of fabric puddled at the base of her spine, leaving her entire back bare.

Low on her back, she bore a small but intricate design drawn in reddish-brown ink. No doubt the henna tattoo she'd mentioned getting. He couldn't resist tracing the image with his forefinger. Her skin was unbelievably soft and he felt her shiver under his touch, making his pulse leap.

He didn't bother to stifle his groan. "You, um, look great."

She looked over her shoulder at him, and though her eyes darkened with desire, her smile teased. "Thanks."

She looked amazing. As if the dress had been made just for her. Something that only made him more aware he'd had to rent his tux. Most of the men she usually dated probably owned their own.

She straightened then tossed him the keys and nodded toward her driveway where the Beemer sat with the top down. "You want to drive?"

Hell, forget about the guys that owned their own tuxes. He was intimidated by the guys who owned cars nice enough to drive her in. His own beat-up work truck didn't qualify.

Still, she was with him. Not any of those other guys who could buy their own tuxes or buy her dinner at a thousand dollars a plate. Him. And that had to count for something.

As he walked her to her car, he automatically slid his hand to the small of her back. He nearly regretted it. Her skin was smooth and warm beneath his hand. With the fabric pooling low on her back, the tips of his fingers brushed against the dimples at the base of her spine.

"A dress this revealing makes a guy wonder what you've got on underneath," he said casually.

"Nothing."

He stilled. "Nothing?" His voice cracked on the word.

She merely smiled. Of their own volition, his eyes dropped to her breasts. He raised his gaze to hers and cocked an eyebrow. Biting innocently on her lip, she shook her head. He looked pointedly to the juncture of her thighs. Again, she shook her head.

"Number six on The List was 'Drop the Drawers.' The article promised it would drive you crazy. Is it working?"

Shaking his head as he opened the passenger door for her, he muttered, "You're killing me, Jess."

She slid into the car, smoothing the skirt of her dress. "Slowly, I hope."

They were several minutes down the road before either of them spoke. For his part, it took all his mental energy to concentrate on keeping the car on the road. Knowing nothing separated the silky fabric from her skin sent his head spinning. Didn't she know he was nervous enough about tonight as it was?

When they reached Main Street, Jessica broke the silence. "Let's not drive through town," she said. "We can take Rock Creek Road. Pick up the highway on the other side of the foothills and be there almost as soon."

That was an exaggeration at best. Taking Rock Creek Road would add a good fifteen minutes onto the drive. But he didn't argue with her. Why not postpone the inevitable?

So he turned left on Main Street instead of right. Drove away from town and from the country club. Away from the social and work obligations they'd both eventually have to return to. Eventually, but not yet.

Rock Creek Road met Main Street just west of town. From there it snaked north through the foothills of the Sierra Nevada. Like all country roads, the lighting was poor to nonexistent. The branches of the trees on either side of the road met overhead, intermittently blocking out the starlight. When the wind was right, the breezes carried the scent of the apple blossoms from the nearby orchards. On one of the hairpin turns, there was room to pull off. The surrounding trees had been trimmed, revealing a spectacular view of the town.

Making the drive, it seemed as if no time had passed. Following the curves of the road, Alex felt eighteen again. Young and stupid with passion. But this time he was stupid with love, as well.

It seemed he'd been waiting his whole life to drive up this road with Jessica beside him in the car. Nothing had ever felt more right.

As they approached the bend in the road, he slowed the car. "Do you want to stop?"

Looking at him from beneath her lashes, she nodded. "You bet."

He slowed the car to a stop, having turned off the road, then angling the car for the best view of the city before setting the parking brake. The surrounding trees were taller than he remembered.

"Funny," he said. "The view's not as impressive as I remember."

"Funny, I didn't think you came here to admire the view."

He laughed. "That's true. But the view helped."

"You sound nervous." She reached out her hand to his then toyed with his fingers where they rested on the gearshift. "Don't tell me you're worried about tonight."

"Nervous? No." *Terrified? Yes.*

Terrified that as soon as they arrived at the gala, he'd do something stupid to embarrass her. Or that he'd insult someone important. That even if he stood in the corner and didn't talk to anyone the whole night, that by the time they left, she'd know the truth about him. That he wasn't really all that different from the dirt-poor, reckless kid he'd been a decade ago. That he had no more right to be with her now than he had then. That she was way out of his league.

"Aren't you going to try to talk me into the back seat?" Her words were bold, but she blushed as she said them.

His control slipped a notch. She looked so lovely in the moonlight. Her hair gleamed, pulled back from her face and twisted into a mass of delicate curls high on the back of her head. Her very skin seemed to glow from within, pale and lovely, pink tingeing her cheeks and the base of her neck.

It'd be so easy to lean over and kiss her. To wipe away her memories of the boy he'd been. But he hesitated before finally forcing himself to ask, "Do you think that's

wise?" He glanced at his watch. "The gala has already
started. We'll be late as it is."

"You're right. It's not wise. Not at all. In fact, it's a very
bad idea."

With a flick of the handle, she swung her car door open.
She climbed out then fumbled for a second with a lever.
Her seat sprang forward. She raised her skirt as she
climbed into the back seat, revealing red high heels, sheer
hose and just a glimpse of garters. She pulled the door
closed behind her before settling into the seat and toeing
off her shoes.

He warred with himself for only a moment, knowing it
would be a very bad idea to show up at this gala fresh from
making love to Jessica in the back seat of her car. But fac-
ing this temptation, logic simply couldn't win out. It took
him mere seconds to join her.

He wanted to pull her immediately into his arms. To
grind her mouth beneath his and to bury himself in her
body. To make her completely his in the only way he knew
how.

He may not have the money or the resources or the
background that she deserved. But he did have this…this
sexual connection to her. The ability to drive her crazy.

It might be all he had going for him. Maybe it wouldn't
be enough. Or maybe it would.

He stopped himself just short of dragging her against
his body. That wasn't how this was done. Up on Rock
Creek Road, in the back seat of a car, a girl needed to be
coaxed. Tempted into doing things she knew she wasn't
supposed to. Push for too much too soon and you'd lose
everything.

So instead of exploring her luscious mouth, he draped
his arm across her shoulder and pulled her to his side. Eas-

ing back against the supple leather of the seat, he pretended to look at the stars.

"Do you know," she mused. "You were the first person I ever heard use the F-word out loud."

"The F-word?" he teased.

She nodded seriously. "Oh, yes. You must have been in the eighth grade. Mr. Menchero, the band teacher, caught you smoking behind the band hall. You told him to F-off."

He twisted slightly in his seat to better watch her face. Each time she said "F," she pursed her lips slightly. Proof that underneath that sex-goddess dress, she was still the judge's proper daughter.

On a hunch he asked, "Jess, have you ever said—" he hesitated, then borrowed her phrasing "—the F-word out loud?"

She scoffed. "Of course—" But her blush gave her away and she admitted, "Not."

Her skin seemed to glow in the moonlight. He couldn't keep himself from touching her. His fingers nearly trembled with need, but he merely stroked her shoulder, down the length of her arm to the inside of her elbow. "How old are you?" he asked. "Twenty-eight?"

She shivered, leaning closer to him. "Twenty-nine."

"Twenty-nine years old and you've never said the F-word?" Unable to resist the lure of her skin any longer, he nuzzled her neck. The scent of her perfume washed over him, no longer as foreign as it had been that first day he'd kissed her, but still exotic. Still intoxicating.

She gasped, then struggled for words. "It's always seemed like such an angry word."

He kissed her neck, her cheek, making his way to her mouth. As he kissed her, her words reached him through a fog of desire. *What was she talking about?*

Her mouth was hot beneath his. Hot and begging. But also, as always, just a little bit prim. That prim little mouth of hers was one of the things that turned him on the most.

That's right. The F-word.

Just the thought of hearing her prim little mouth say that word out loud made him hard.

He pulled her closer, dragging her half across his body. As he cupped her breasts, he murmured, "You're right. It can be an angry word." His hands found the open back of her dress. Pulling her even closer, he reveled in the softness of her skin. "But it can also be a sexy word."

She pulled away from his kiss, her expression a curious mixture of desire and wide-eyed surprise. "A sexy word?"

"Oh, yeah." He hooked his hands on her thighs and pulled her onto his lap so that she straddled him. "Sexy. Hot. And dirty." He bucked his hips against her. "Isn't that what you want, Jess? Sex that's hot and dirty?"

Biting down on her lip, she smiled, her eyes alight with enthusiasm. She twisted, reaching for her purse, which lay on the console between the front seats. From the red beaded bag, she pulled a single condom.

Oh, yes, this was what she wanted. This was what he could give her. Hot and dirty sex. A quick tussle in the back of a car up on Rock Creek Road.

The red satin of her skirt draped over them. He slid his hands beneath the fabric to her silk-encased legs. The stockings were smooth beneath his palms, her skin hot.

His fingers found the straps of her garter belt. The exquisite flesh of her thighs trembled beneath his touch as he ran his hands up the back of her legs to her bare buttocks. She hadn't lied about not wearing any underwear.

Groaning, he squeezed his eyes closed, desperate for

control. He sucked in deep breaths, one after the other. Even as he struggled to control his desire, he couldn't control his hands, which seemed to mindlessly explore her sensitive skin and the tender folds between her legs.

When he felt her hands unfastening his pants, his eyes flew open. In seconds she'd freed his erection and, with trembling fingers, eased the condom down its length.

He searched her expression in the moonlight. Her lips were red and glistening, her eyelids lowered, her gaze dazed by passion.

She massaged his penis through the condom, her hand hot and eager. She began to lower herself onto his length, but he gripped her hips, holding her above him.

"Not yet," he gasped.

She moaned in protest, her eyes fluttering open.

"Tell me what you want."

"I want you," she said simply.

He wasn't even inside her yet, but already he could feel his orgasm building low in his belly. It took all of his will to hold back. "What do you want me to do?"

"I want you to make love to me."

"No, Jess, this isn't making love. Making love is tender and sweet. This is hot and dirty."

Her eyes flashed with frustration, but then she caught on to the game and she smiled. "I want you to F-word me."

His fingers found the nub of her desire. Stroking her with his thumb, he insisted, "Say it. Come on, Jess."

She jerked and trembled at his touch. His body strained toward hers. Bracing her palms on his shoulders, she leaned over and whispered the words in his ear, demanding what she wanted. He surged up into her, gasping in relief. Driving them both over the edge.

But as he held her trembling in his arms, he realized

he'd lied. Whatever kick he'd once gotten out of the idea of nailing Jessica Sumners, the town's good girl, had long since given way to something much more complicated. With her, even when sex was hot and dirty, it was still making love.

17

As Alex watched Jessica walk across the floor of the country club's main ballroom, for the first time in his life, he felt completely at peace with himself.

He stood listening to one of the city council members— a guy who'd been friends with Tomas back in high school— but his attention was focused entirely on Jessica. She looked breathtaking, with her body encased in that amazing red dress, her blond hair now loose around her shoulders.

When she'd walked through the door, she'd had the attention of every man in the room. But that wasn't the only reason he was glad he had her by his side. She'd worked the crowd like a pro. Remembering everyone's names. Asking about their children and relatives. Their businesses and hobbies.

Conversational sleight of hand, she'd called it. Except now that he saw it up close, he realized it was more than that. She really listened to people. Really cared about them.

That surprised him, even though it probably shouldn't have. He should have known by now there was more to Jessica than met the eye.

The people at the gala surprised him, as well. He'd always pictured the country club filled with rich snobs. People in tuxedoes and glittering gowns looking down their noses at him.

It wasn't like that at all. Half the town had turned up for this thing. He saw people he'd gone to high school with or known as a child as well as people he'd done business with since he'd returned—Hank Hansen, who owned the hardware store, and even Steve Foscoe from the lumberyard. Not necessarily rich people or snobby people. Just people.

As he looked around the room, most of the men, like him, looked a little uncomfortable surrounded by this wealth and glamour. He saw very few men who looked rich enough to own their tuxes and none, other than her father, looked as though they could truly afford these expensive fund-raiser dinners.

He hadn't wanted Jessica to have to settle for a guy like him, a guy who worked in construction. He had worried so much about all the things he couldn't give Jessica. But, really, what could any of these guys give her that he couldn't?

Sure, some of them made more money. A couple of them maybe even could afford those thousand-dollar-a-plate dinners. But had she ever said she wanted that? No, she hadn't. But she had said she wanted him.

And even if he didn't have money or a prestigious job, there was one thing he could offer her that no other man in this room could. His love.

He knew without even a flicker of doubt that he loved her in a way no other man could. And if she was willing, he'd spend the rest of his life making sure she never settled for anything less than she deserved.

He searched the room, wanting to find Jessica, who'd somehow disappeared in the crowd. Needing to be with her, even if he couldn't immediately tell her how he felt. But before he could find her, Senator Sumners cornered him.

As soon as they were alone, he pinned Alex with a steely stare. It was the same emotionless look Alex remembered from the courtroom. And now that he thought about, it was the look Jessica had given him the few times she'd wanted him to keep his distance. The familiarity of it was calming. Sort of.

"It seems you're dating my daughter," the senator said flatly.

Alex wasn't sure if he'd heard disdain in the statement or merely imagined it. He tapped down the barest instinct to shoot off some smart-ass comeback. "Yes, sir, I am."

The senator's eyes narrowed for a second, no doubt gauging his sincerity. Finally his expression relaxed infinitesimally. "You've learned some manners since you were last in my courtroom."

He'd had manners then, he just hadn't seen the point in using them.

"Well." The senator cleared his throat. "No doubt Jessica's led you to expect some kind of inquisition from me."

"Actually, she has."

"Her mother and I tend to be a little overprotective where Jessica is concerned. Because of her good nature, we haven't wanted people to take advantage of her."

"Jessica is one of the most stubborn people I've ever met. I can't imagine anyone taking advantage of her."

The senator frowned. "No, perhaps you can't. Nevertheless—"

"Let me save you some time, Senator. This is the part of the conversation where you warn me off. You remind me that I can't give her all the things she's used to. Point out that we're from different worlds. You ask me to stay away from her. You wrap it up with a big speech about how I'm just not good enough for her."

Jessica's father stared blankly at him for a minute, then asked, "Are you done?"

"No, not yet." He probably should be, but he wasn't. He'd been expecting this speech since he'd walked into the ballroom tonight—hell, he'd been giving it to himself since he'd walked into her house—but in the end, he could think of only one response. "The thing is, sir, you're right. I'm not good enough for her. But the way I see it, who is? I'm not rich like some of the other men in this room, and I can't give her some of the things they can, but I can make her happy. Because I love her more than any other man ever will. And I think she cares about me, too."

"That was quite a speech." The senator studied him with a raised eyebrow. "Did you practice that long?"

"Ever since we walked in." Alex chuckled as he said it, the sound more nervous than amused. He hated standing in front of this man and feeling judged by him.

The senator nodded. "Well, I've been practicing mine a bit longer than that."

Now it was Alex's turn to raise his eyebrows.

"If I've been hard on the men my daughter dates, it's because I only want her to be happy. If you honestly think you're the man who can do that, you're welcome to give it a try. But I have to warn you, you were right about her being stubborn. If you really love her, I'm not the one you have to convince. She is."

"OH, JESSICA, what *were* you thinking?"

Jessica glanced down at her watch before turning to face her mother. Fifty-two minutes. She braced herself for the faux motherly embrace as a cloud of Chanel No. 5 surrounded her.

"Almost an hour, Mom. You're losing your touch."

Her mother blinked, managing to look both innocent and surprised. "I don't know what you mean."

"Fifty-two minutes. That's the amount of time that's passed since Alex and I walked in the door. Frankly, I would have thought you'd have rushed over to make some snide comment a lot sooner than that."

The surprised innocence flashed briefly to annoyance before settling into an expression of vague hurt. No doubt in case anyone walked close enough to overhear them. Her mother had shanghaied her on her way back from the rest room, which meant they were close to the flow of traffic.

"Really, Jessica, I can't imagine why you'd think I'd do such a thing…but now that you mention it, I was surprised that you didn't bring that nice man you were dating from work."

Biting back her frustration, she said, "I didn't bring him, because we broke up. Quite a while ago, actually. And you know that, because I've mentioned it twice. So why don't you just say whatever it is you're going to say about Alex and get it over with?"

Her mother sighed. "Yes, I know you broke up. I just had hoped you might have worked things out."

"I didn't want to work things out. I knew after two dates he wasn't the kind of guy I'd want to have a relationship with."

"But at least you would have had something in common with him and—"

"He wasn't someone I wanted to spend the rest of my life with. He wasn't someone I could have loved."

"So you're saying you love this Alex person?"

For an instant Jessica thought her heart had stopped beating. Was that what she was saying?

Across the crowded dance floor, her eyes sought Alex. He stood waiting in line at the bar, talking to her father. Both men seemed surprisingly relaxed. Apparently, Alex was fairing better than she was.

He looked comfortable, calm and unbelievably handsome. No one would guess he'd been nervous about coming here tonight. She knew, but only because she'd sensed it in the car. Sensed his desperation when they'd had sex. Sensed it and knew him well enough to understand why he was nervous.

Yes, it had been hard for him to come here tonight. To walk back into the country club he'd helped his uncle remodel. To face all the people—her father included—who'd made things difficult for him. And yet he'd done it. Not—she suddenly realized—because it would be good for his career, but because she'd asked him to.

From across the room, he glanced in her direction and caught her looking at him. His lips curved into a wry smile before he pointedly turned his attention back to the conversation, as if to show her he was doing his best.

"Are you?" her mother asked again.

She pulled her eyes away from Alex to stare blankly at her mother. "I don't know," she answered honestly. "I certainly didn't plan to fall in love with him."

Talk about the understatement of the century. She'd planned to have nothing more than a wild fling with him. Great sex, big passion and a chance to check number one off The List. Nothing more.

Her mother sighed in resignation. "Well, if you are, I don't suppose there's much we can do about it now, is there?"

"Sorry to disappoint you."

The annoyance in her mother's gaze was back. "Look,

dear, I know you like to see me as cold, heartless and manipulative. But I genuinely do want you to be happy. And I just can't imagine you being happy with someone like him. I never could."

Now her mother had her complete attention. "What's that supposed to mean?"

"I just always thought he was wrong for you."

"'Always'? What do you mean you 'always' thought? Alex and I have been together for less than three weeks." And that was being generous. "And you didn't even know we were together until tonight."

"I don't mean now, of course. I mean back when you were in high school."

"Now you've really lost me. There was nothing between Alex and me back then."

"Dear, this is a very small town. You should know as well as anyone how difficult it is to keep a secret. That combined with all those notes he used to write you... Surely you didn't think we didn't know about the two of you."

"Notes?" She thought of the notes they'd sent each other for those few brief weeks in high school. Notes even her best friend Mattie hadn't known about. "How did you know about the notes?"

"Mrs. Nguyen found them in your bedroom and brought them to me."

Shaking her head in confusion and wishing she could shake her mother instead, she said, "And from a handful of notes you and Daddy concluded Alex and I were dating? I barely knew him back in high school. We only spoke a handful of times. We exchanged maybe a dozen notes. That was it."

"So you weren't secretly dating him?"

"No. Why would you even think that?"

This time, her mother looked genuinely surprised. "Well, when he and that Higgins boy fought over you, your father and I just assumed…"

"Alex and Albert Higgins never fought over…" Her voice trailed off as she considered it. "Did they?"

She looked to her mom for answers, even though she knew only Alex could provide them.

Nevertheless her mother nodded. "I'm afraid they did. You didn't know?"

"No, I had no…wait a second, was that why Daddy 'suggested' Alex leave town? Because you two thought Alex and I were secretly dating?"

Her mother fumed and at least had the grace to look ashamed. "Your father believed it would be for the best. For you and for him. The Higginses were prepared to press charges against him and he never could have afforded a decent lawyer. It seemed like the best solution for all involved."

Appalled at her father's questionable ethics, she snapped, "For you and the Higginses maybe, but not—"

"Yes, for Alex, too," her mother interrupted her. "He'd been arrested several times before—he'd been on probation, for goodness' sakes. But he was over eighteen this time, a legal adult. If he'd been charged with assault and battery—"

"So instead, everything was just swept under the carpet and hushed up. Do you have any idea how ethically questionable this is?" Shaking her head, she threw up her hands in exasperation. "Of course you do. You're the wife of a judge. Of a senator."

Her mother stiffened, a hint of indignation creeping into her voice. "Your father did it to protect you—"

"From what? From nothing. There was nothing going on between Alex and me."

"Your father didn't know that."

"Well, he could have asked! I guess that's Daddy at his dictatorial worst." Almost pleading for understanding, she looked to her mother. "Why didn't you ask?"

Staring off into the crowd as if looking into the past, her mother sighed, shaking her head. "I don't know. I guess we thought we were protecting you. You were always such a good girl. So serious. So well behaved. And a boy like Alex Moreno? Always getting into trouble. Well, we could see why you would be drawn to each other."

Of course, Jessica had to admit, they'd been right about that. For her part at least. She had been drawn to Alex even back then.

"Your father thought it would be better if the whole thing just went away. He was worried that if he confronted you about it, you'd do something stupid. Young love can be very stupid, you know."

But she didn't know. She'd never been in love when she was young. The question was, was she in love now?

After a few minutes of awkward silence, her mother excused herself and disappeared, leaving Jessica alone with her thoughts.

Her gaze automatically found Alex in the crowd. He'd ditched her father and appeared to be trying to make his way over to her, a drink in each hand, although he'd been stopped and drawn into yet another conversation.

She hadn't been particularly worried about how he would handle himself tonight, but it was nice to know he was doing just fine without her. Apparently he didn't need her help, after all.

As she turned to make her way back to the table they

shared with Brad and Mattie, she caught a glimpse of the man she'd been secretly looking for all night long: Martin Schaffer, the owner of the Hotel Mimosa. It had taken her several phone calls to convince Martin to drive in for the gala, but since he was the last man Moreno Construction had worked for, she was sure it would be worth it. She'd done some additional poking around online and learned that Martin was active in historical preservation groups across the state.

If anyone could convince the members of the historical society that Alex could do the courthouse remodel, he could.

As she made her way across the crowded room, she renewed her determination to help Alex. His relationship with her may have hurt him in the past, but now she'd finally found a way to really help his career.

Martin greeted her warmly when she approached him, going so far as to pull her into an enthusiastic bear hug. She laughed awkwardly as she pulled away.

"Oh, look, I've embarrassed you." He swatted at her arm. "But I feel like I know you already. Besides anyone who'd go to such great lengths to help out Alex is practically family already."

"So, you know Alex pretty well, then?"

"He's like a brother. But one that knows how to use a hammer. He's hands down the best general contractor I've ever worked with. I'm itching to talk him up to these old biddies you're worried about. But after that long drive, first I'll need a drink. Then I'll want to say hello to the boy himself. He knows I'm coming?"

"It's a surprise," she explained as they made their way across the room to where she'd last seen Alex.

"Excellent." Martin clapped his hands together. "You know, I was surprised when you called."

"Well, I imagine." After all, how could he have anticipated her calling?

"I mean, I'm just tickled pink he's up for a job like this courthouse of yours, but I certainly didn't see it coming."

"What do you mean, a job like this?" she asked with trepidation. "I thought the job he did renovating the Hotel Mimosa was even bigger than this."

"It was. I just remember how glad he was it was done. He said he couldn't wait to move home and scale things back a bit. Have a personal life for once." He slanted her a suggestive look. "Which I guess he's been doing."

"Hmm," she said noncommittally. Forming an actual response was completely beyond her because she was still trying to sort out exactly what Martin's words meant.

Alex didn't want any more big jobs? Which meant he didn't want the job at the courthouse. So why hadn't he told her?

But here he was, dutifully schmoozing with everyone in town, making the best of a situation he'd never wanted to be in. All so he could get a job he didn't want. All because she'd pushed him into it.

She felt as if Martin had pulled the rug out from under her, and it was just one shock too many. She continued to walk alongside Martin, introducing him to all the right people and saying all the right things, but her thoughts continued to swirl around this problem with Alex.

After tonight, she certainly understood why he'd been so sure a relationship with her would hurt his business. Mere rumors—false rumors, for that matter—about their relationship had already had a huge impact on his life.

No wonder he'd tried to keep her at arms' length. Not that it had done him any good. She'd been so sure of herself, she'd dismissed all of his concerns. Just ignored them.

And she'd accused her father of being dictatorial. It seemed she was more like him than she wanted to admit.

And unlike him, as well. She still couldn't believe he'd done something so unethical, so questionable. That knowledge skewed everything she knew about herself.

Her mother was right. All her life she had been such a good girl. She'd always assumed it was just part of being the judge's daughter. As though it were a trait she'd inherited or something. Or worse still, something the town had inflicted on her. But now she realized it wasn't just a good-girl image. It was who she was.

Her father's actions horrified her. They offended her. How very good girl-ish of her. How very moral.

It seemed, at the end of the day, she wasn't *Saucy* after all. She was, in fact, exactly what she'd been trying to avoid being all along…a very good girl. Moral, upstanding and—when it came to some things—very proper.

She sighed with resignation. So her mother thought young love could be stupid? Well, adult love wasn't shaping up to be very smart, either. She couldn't change who she was. Not even for Alex. Oh, she'd tried to be saucy, tried to shed that good-girl image, but she couldn't change who she was deep down.

She realized that now. And sooner or later, he would, too.

With that thought sitting heavy in her gut, she once again looked for Alex, only this time, something else caught her attention. Brad and Mattie, dancing together.

Leading her across the dance floor to the old Etta James favorite, "At Last," Brad swung her around and whispered something in her ear that made her giggle and blush before he spun her out the length of his arm. It was a perfect, movie-worthy moment.

And they both looked so happy. So perfectly matched to each other, so completely in love. In that instant, it seemed hard to believe that they hadn't always been in love. That every moment of their lives hadn't been leading up to this one.

But then, maybe they had.

Her breath seemed to catch in her chest as she watched them dance. Suddenly she knew what she wanted.

Yes, she wanted passion. But she didn't want just passionate sex from Alex. She wanted passionate love.

Suddenly she knew what her biggest fear was. It wasn't loving Alex, it was losing him. Not being with him, not living her life with him, was by far the scariest thing she could imagine. Nevertheless, she'd have to give him up.

When she'd started this journey to becoming a *Saucy* woman, she'd promised herself that she'd never again settle for less than she deserved. She deserved to be with a man who loved her, and he didn't. He couldn't love her because he didn't even know her. She'd just spent the past two weeks convincing him she was someone other than who she really was.

18

"Do you even want the job renovating the courthouse?"

"Sure, but—"

"No, I mean, do you *really* want it? All this time, I've been pushing, thinking it was what you wanted, but now, I'm not so sure."

She sounded so confused and unsure, so unlike herself, that it worried him. "Jess, what's up?"

She stared out the window, not even glancing in his direction as he navigated the winding roads back to her house.

"I just assumed I knew what was best for you. I was so sure I was right. I just kept pushing..." Her voice broke and he heard her clear her throat before continuing. "But tonight when I was talking to Martin, I realized you don't even want the job at the courthouse. After the amazing work you did on the Hotel Mimosa, you had it made, you could have gone anywhere and gotten any job, but instead you came home."

Now she did turn to look at him, and it made him nervous, because he knew what she was about to say and he knew he couldn't lie to her.

"I thought you'd come home so you could show everyone how successful you'd been, but that wasn't it, was it?" She didn't wait for him to answer, but plunged ahead.

"You came home to avoid success, because success made you feel guilty, like you were betraying your parents. That's the real reason why you never worked on a bid for the job at the courthouse. It wasn't just that you thought you wouldn't get it, it's that you didn't want it."

He kept his gaze pinned to the road, trying to think of something to say, but when she asked him point-blank, the words seemed to stick a little in his throat.

"I'm right, aren't I?"

"Maybe." He pulled his hand off the gearshift long enough to run his fingers through his hair. "Yeah, I guess that was part of it. But I don't think even I knew that when I first moved back. I wanted to be closer to my family. And I was tired of running away from my past."

"You should have said something."

"It seemed important to you." He hadn't wanted to disappoint her. And he'd liked the way she stood up for him. No one had ever done that before. Besides, if he'd told her point-blank, she probably wouldn't have hired him to remodel her kitchen. Then he wouldn't have had an excuse to see her every day. To spend time with her.

"Right. It seemed important to me. It *was* important to me. But only because I thought it was what you wanted. I was just so sure I was right, I never stopped to ask you what you wanted."

He didn't like where this was going. When he turned the corner onto her street, relief flooded him. As soon as he set the emergency break in her driveway, he reached for her.

But she flattened herself against the door, just out of his reach.

"Jess, you want to know what's important to me? You are. You're the only thing that matters. I do care about the job at the courthouse. I want it because you want me to have it. I want it for you. I lo—"

She practically lunged across the car, pressing her fingers against his lips, trapping the words in his mouth.

"Don't say that. You don't really mean it. You just think you do."

Huh?

He didn't even get the chance to ask her what the hell she was talking about, because she kept talking.

"You may think you care about me, but you're wrong. You only think that because I've made you believe it."

He grabbed her wrist and pulled her fingers from his mouth. "What are you talking about?"

"I was so sure I could make you want me, that we'd be good together, that I didn't even stop to think about what you would want."

"*You* are what I want."

"No, I'm not. Not really. Don't you remember what you said? You wanted someone light and casual. Someone playful and wild. Someone saucy. I'm none of those things."

"Jessica that was just a random list. That's not what I really want."

But she ignored him completely. "I made you believe I was those things because I wanted to be with you. Just like I pushed you to do the bid for the courthouse because I believe it would make you happy. I was so sure I knew how to fix everything and now I've just mucked everything up."

"But, Jessica—"

"You don't have to worry anymore. I'm through messing up your life. I've decided to go back to Sweden."

"Sweden?" What the hell was she talking about?

"Yes." Her voice hardened with her resolve. "When I was there on business, the company I worked with offered me a job. It's a great position."

All he could do was repeat numbly, "Sweden?"

"This will be for the best. I know it will."

And with that, she threw open the car and ran to her house in a flurry of red silk. For a moment he considered going after her right there and then, but he wasn't sure it would do any good.

She had it all worked out in her head. Boy, talk about mucking things up.

She thought she had it all figured out. But she hadn't counted on one thing. He didn't just think he was in love with the woman she was pretending to be. He knew he was in love with the woman she was.

JESSICA SHUT HER front door behind her, locked the dead bolt and leaned her back against the closed door. She stood in the darkened hall with her head ducked, a heavy lock of her hair hanging in front of her eyes, one hand clenching the beaded purse she'd carried, the other grasping the lone house key she'd kept tucked inside. Holding her breath, she listened for the sound of his truck starting up and pulling away from her house.

Any second now she'd hear it. He'd be mad—furious maybe. The engine would roar to life, he'd slam the truck into gear and tear down the street. The way he used to in his Camaro all those years ago.

She heard the truck start and, when it didn't pull away, she pictured him sitting there. Mulling over her words. Replaying them in his mind, just as she was doing.

Any second now he'd realize the truth of what she'd said, put the truck in gear and drive away. Maybe out of her life forever.

She squeezed her eyes closed, summoning the courage to let him go, when what she really wanted to do was throw the door open and run after him.

This is for the best, she told herself sternly. *For you and him.*

Chanting those words over and over, she dropped her purse and the house key onto the console table by the door and walked down the hall, toward her bedroom. Her boring cream bedroom, which perfectly matched her boring bland house and her boring bland life.

Then she heard the one noise she hadn't expected. The sound of her front door opening behind her. She stilled, held her breath and then spun around.

Alex stood, framed by the open doorway, dangling her car keys from his forefinger.

"Next time you plan a dramatic exit," he said lightly, leaning his shoulder against the doorjamb, "you might want to get your car keys back first."

He tossed the keys in her direction, but she didn't react fast enough and they landed at her feet with a clatter.

She'd just ended their relationship and he was teasing her?

"You brought me back my keys," she said numbly.

"Yep."

His mocking smile wore away at her already frail self-control. "I just broke up with you—I just told you I was moving to Sweden—and you brought me back my keys."

He nodded. "Yeah, that about sums it up."

Shock gave way to stirrings of anger. "I just broke up with you and you're not upset at all. Are you?"

His shoulders shifted beneath the tux jacket as he shrugged indifferently. "No, not really."

"What is wrong with you?" She heard her voice rising toward hysteria, but seemed unable to curb it. "Did our relationship mean nothing to you? Do you feel noth—"

Before she could finish her outburst, he propelled himself away from the door and toed it closed in one quick motion. A second later he pulled her into his arms, molded her body to his and kissed her.

His lips were hot and hard against hers, his mouth demanding, urgent and filled with emotion. Not light and casual emotion, either. Not playful or fun. It was a kiss full of dark possessiveness and layered with complexity.

By the time he pulled away from her, she knew for sure that he definitely felt more than nothing for her.

He stared down at her in the dimly lit hall. A single table lamp in the other room cast a shadow across his face, obscuring his expression. But—despite the intensity of his kiss—his tone was teasing when he said, "You know, it's rude to interrupt someone when they're talking."

"It—it is?"

"Absolutely. I'd have thought you of all people would know that."

"I—I do, but—"

"Then let me finish what I was saying out there in the car. I love you, Jessica."

"But—"

"The woman you are. Stubborn, serious, honest and fair. I love it when you try to be light and playful. I love it when you fail. I love it when you're naughty, but I love it more when you're good."

His gaze darkened as he stared down at her. His fingers

traced the line of her jaw down to her chin where he chucked her lightly. "I love it when you push me harder than I would push myself. Being with you makes me want more than I would want on my own. It was like that even back in high school, when I'd spend hours working on those notes so you'd think I was smart. I even love the way you get all bossy and try to make decisions for everyone else, but I'm not going to let you get away with it this time."

"But don't you see? That's not what I'm doing this time. I'm backing off. I'm letting it go."

That was, after all, the phrase he'd used over and over when she'd pressed him to get his bid completed for the courthouse.

But he shook his head as if chastising her. "No, you're not."

"But—"

"Do you believe I love you?"

"No, you just think you do because—"

"So you didn't believe me when I said I didn't want to put in a bid on the courthouse, and you don't believe me now when I say I love you. It's not different. You're still doing it."

"But—" And damn it, he was right. What she was doing now *wasn't* any different. Except that she *knew* she was right about this...just like she'd been sure before.

With a frustrated sigh, she asked, "So what do we do?"

He pulled her toward his chest, laughing as he comforted her. "You're just going to have to learn to believe me when I say I love you just as you are. Not lighter. Not more playful. Not more wild."

Her breath caught in her chest as relief welled up inside her. "I—I'll try?"

She felt his arm tighten across her back and a tension she hadn't even realized he'd been feeling begin to dissipate from his muscles.

"You know now would be a great time to tell me you love me, too."

She pulled back just enough to look up into his eyes. "I do love you, too. You don't doubt that do you?"

"Good, because you told me over and over again not to settle for less than I deserve. I'm still not convinced I deserve you, but you are what I want. And I want all of you. Your whole heart, your whole mind, forever. And I don't want to settle for anything less than that."

Her happiness blossomed within her. "That works out well. Because I don't want to, either."

She rose up onto her toes as if to kiss him, but he stopped her just shy of it. "I might as well say this now, since I'm on a roll. I don't want to move to Sweden."

Blinking in confusion, she said, "Huh?"

"If you want that job in Sweden, you should take it. I'll even go there with you—hell, people in Sweden need decks or saunas or something—but I'd much rather stay right here."

"I don't want to move to Sweden, either. I just didn't want to be here without you."

He nuzzled her neck with his lips and, at his touch, a shiver of anticipation curled its way through her body. She pressed herself closer to him, leaning up to whisper a suggestion in his ear. This time, she didn't hesitate to use a very dirty word. There were lots of words she'd heard and never used. Lots of things she'd never tried. A lot of them were naughty words, words she'd never said out loud. But some of them were words she'd used all her life but never understood.

Words like commitment, marriage, love and happiness.

Epilogue

JESSICA WENT TRIBAL for her wedding day, too, the backs of her hands painted in a traditional Mendhi wedding design, to signify her transformation from fiancée to wife. On her left hand she wore the antique pearl ring he'd scoured the shops to find. It wasn't the huge diamond some other guy might have been able to afford, but it suited Jessica perfectly. Besides, he'd wanted to replace the pearl necklace she'd given to Miranda.

Jessica's mother sniffed with disapproval when she saw the designs. But then again, she liked almost nothing about Jessica's and Alex's wedding. And the Mendhi was the least of her complaints, given the fact that they weren't even wed in a church, but rather in the just-completed foyer of the courthouse.

Alex had had to push to get the foyer ready in time, but he'd managed it, nevertheless.

Jessica's sole concession to her mother was to have the reception at the country club. And as Alex led her across the dance floor while "At Last" played in the background, she whispered into his ear, "I hate to admit it, but my mother was right. I'm glad we had the reception here."

"We had to," he murmured back. "It was the only place big enough to hold everyone. I told you everyone in Palo Verde loves you."

She smiled into his neck. "They love you, too, you know."

He snorted. "Now that we're married, they do."

But if he was honest, the town had warmed up to him long before their wedding or even their engagement. Sure, there were a few people, like Mrs. Higgins, who still gave him the cold shoulder occasionally, but even she'd begun to warm up once he'd started working on the courthouse.

Dancing with Jessica now, it seemed as if he'd always been as much a part of this town as she had. Surrounded by her family and his, as well as half the town, it was hard to remember why he'd stayed away so long, when clearly, this had always been home.

"Funny," he mused. "It feels like my whole life has been leading up to this moment."

As soon as he heard how cheesy the words sounded, he wished he could take them back.

But then Jessica looked up at him, her head tilted to the side in that way she had, a slightly bemused expression on her face. "That's exactly how I feel."

Her words reminded him all over again why he loved her so much. She was the one person in the world he could say anything to. She always had been.

Harlequin on Location

hot tips

Wherever your dream date location,
pick a setting and a time that won't be
interrupted by your daily responsibilities.
This is a special time together. Here are
a few hopelessly romantic settings to
inspire you—they might as well be ripped
right out of a Harlequin romance novel!

Bad weather can be so good.
Take a walk together after a fresh snowfall or when it's just stopped
raining. Pick a snowball (or a puddle) fight, and see how long it takes
to get each other soaked to the bone. Then enjoy drying off in front of
a fire, or perhaps surrounded by lots and lots of candles with yummy
hot chocolate to warm things up.

Candlelight dinner for two…in the bedroom.
Romantic music and candles will instantly transform the place you
sleep into a cozy little love nest, perfect for nibbling. Why not lay
down a blanket and open a picnic basket at the foot of your bed? Or
set a beautiful table with your finest dishes and glowing candles to set
the mood. Either way, a little bubbly and lots of light finger foods will
make this a meal to remember.

A Wild and Crazy Weeknight.
Do something unpredictable…on a weeknight straight from work.
Go to an art opening, a farm-team baseball game, the local playhouse,
a book signing by an author or a jazz club—anything but the humdrum
blockbuster movie. There's something very romantic about being
a little wild and crazy—or at least out of the ordinary—that will
bring out the flirt in both of you. And you won't be able to resist
thinking about each other in anticipation of your hot date…or telling
everyone the day after.

Are you a chocolate lover? ♥

Try WALDORF CHOCOLATE FONDUE— a true chocolate decadence ♥ ♥

♥ ♥

While many couples choose to dine out on Valentine's Day, one of the most romantic things you can do for your sweetheart is to prepare an elegant meal—right in the comfort of your own home.

Harlequin asked John Doherty, executive chef at the Waldorf-Astoria Hotel in New York City, for his recipe for seduction—the famous Waldorf Chocolate Fondue....

WALDORF CHOCOLATE FONDUE
Serves 6-8

2 cups water
½ cup corn syrup
I cup sugar
8 oz dark bitter chocolate, chopped
I pound cake (can be purchased in supermarket)
2–3 cups assorted berries
2 cups pineapple
½ cup peanut brittle

Bring water, corn syrup and sugar to a boil in a medium-size pot. Turn off the heat and add the chopped chocolate. Strain and pour into fondue pot. Cut cake and fruit into cubes and 1-inch pieces. Place fondue pot in the center of a serving plate, arrange cake, fruit and peanut brittle around pot. Serve with forks.

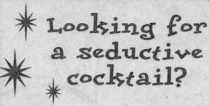

Looking for a seductive cocktail?

hot tips

Try *Ero-Desiac*—
a dazzling martini

With its warm apricot walls yet cool atmosphere, Verlaine is quickly becoming one of New York's hottest nightspots. Verlaine created a light, subtle yet seductive martini for Harlequin: the Ero-Desiac. Sake warms the heart and soul, while jasmine and passion fruit ignite the senses....

The Ero-Desiac

Combine vodka, sake, passion fruit puree and jasmine tea. Mix and shake. Strain into a martini glass, then rest pomegranate syrup on the edge of the martini glass and drizzle the syrup down the inside of the glass.

An Invitation for Love

hot tips

Find a special way to invite your guy into your Harlequin Moment. Letting him know you're looking for a little romance will help put his mind on the same page as yours. In fact, if you do it right, he won't be able to stop thinking about you until he sees you again!

Send him a long-stemmed rose tied to an invitation that leaves a lot up to the imagination.

♥

Autograph a favorite photo of you and tape it on the appointed day in his day planner. Block out the hours he'll be spending with you.

♥

Send him a local map and put an *X* on the place you want him to meet you. Write: "I'm lost without you. Come find me. Tonight at 8." Use magazine cutouts and photographs to paste images of romance and the two of you all over the map.

♥

Send him something personal that he'll recognize as yours to his office. Write: "If found, please return. Owner offers reward to anyone returning item by 7:30 on Saturday night." Don't sign the card.

If you enjoyed what you just read,
then we've got an offer you can't resist!

Take 2 bestselling
love stories FREE!
Plus get a FREE surprise gift!

Clip this page and mail it to Harlequin Reader Service®

IN U.S.A.	IN CANADA
3010 Walden Ave.	P.O. Box 609
P.O. Box 1867	Fort Erie, Ontario
Buffalo, N.Y. 14240-1867	L2A 5X3

YES! Please send me 2 free Blaze™ novels and my free surprise gift. After receiving them, if I don't wish to receive anymore, I can return the shipping statement marked cancel. If I don't cancel, I will receive 4 brand-new novels each month, before they're available in stores! In the U.S.A., bill me at the bargain price of $3.99 plus 25¢ shipping and handling per book and applicable sales tax, if any*. In Canada, bill me at the bargain price of $4.47 plus 25¢ shipping and handling per book and applicable taxes**. That's the complete price and a savings of at least 10% off the cover prices—what a great deal! I understand that accepting the 2 free books and gift places me under no obligation ever to buy any books. I can always return a shipment and cancel at any time. Even if I never buy another book from Harlequin, the 2 free books and gift are mine to keep forever.

150 HDN DZ9K
350 HDN DZ9L

Name	(PLEASE PRINT)	
Address	Apt.#	
City	State/Prov.	Zip/Postal Code

Not valid to current Harlequin Blaze™ subscribers.

Want to try two free books from another series?
Call 1-800-873-8635 or visit www.morefreebooks.com.

* Terms and prices subject to change without notice. Sales tax applicable in N.Y.
** Canadian residents will be charged applicable provincial taxes and GST.
All orders subject to approval. Offer limited to one per household.
® and ™ are registered trademarks owned and used by the trademark owner and or its licensee.

BLZ04R   ©2004 Harlequin Enterprises Limited.

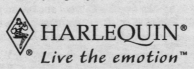

It's hot...and out of control!

Don't miss these bold and ultrasexy books!

BUILDING A BAD BOY by Colleen Collins
Harlequin Temptation #1016
March 2005

WARM & WILLING by Kate Hoffmann
Harlequin Temptation #1017
April 2005

HER LAST TEMPTATION by Leslie Kelly
Harlequin Temptation #1028
June 2005

Look for these books at your favorite retail outlet.

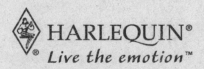

HARLEQUIN®
Live the emotion™

www.eHarlequin.com

HTHEAT